Spring Seeds

At Home in Pennsylvania Amish Country 2

Karen Anna Vogel

He restores my soul

Spring Seeds: At Home in Pennsylvania Amish County

Contact the author on Facebook at:

www.facebook.com/VogelReaders

Learn more the author at: www.karenannavogel.com

Visit her blog, Amish Crossings, at

www.karenannavogel.blogspot.com

ISBN-13:978-1717385673
ISBN-10: 1717385672

:

Dedicated to Christin,

My daughter and friend.

This book was written during many Jonah Days;

Your care and kindness made writing possible.

Amore!

TABLE OF CONTENTS

Amish – English Dictionary

Amish-English Dictionary

How Pennsylvania Dutch overflows into Western Pennsylvanian slang.

"To be" or not to be, that is the question. Folks in Western PA, along with local Amish, do not use "to be". It's not "The car needs *to be* washed." We simply say, "The car needs washed." This is only one example. This book is full of similar "grammar errors" but tries to be authentic to how people talk in our "neck of the woods."

Ach – oh
Boppli – baby
Bopplin -babies
Daed - dad
Danki – thank you
Dochder -daughter
Eck table – a table set in a corner for the bride and groom
Ferhoodled – Messed up, confusing
Gmay – community or church
Grossdaddi - grandfather
Grossmammi - grandmother
Gut – good
Jah - yes
Kapp- cap; Amish women's head covering
Kinner – children
Mamm – mom
Nee- no
Ordnung - A set of rules for Amish, Old Order Mennonite and Conservative Mennonite living. Ordnung is the German word for order, discipline, rule, arrangement, organization, or system.
Rumspringa – running around years, starting at sixteen, when Amish youth experience the outsiders' way of life before joining the church.
Wunderbar – wonderful
Yinz – You all or you two, slang found in Western Pennsylvania among the Amish and those who speak Pittsburghese.

Chapter 1

The wind whipped across the rolling hills of Punxsutawney as it plummeted to ten degrees, but my best friend's cozy little wedding warmed my heart. Lena looked ever so radiant in this little room with a crackling fire and a close circle of friends.

I held fast to my husband's hand, remembering our own wedding a few years back. How outspoken I was for an Amish woman. *I proposed!* I didn't come out and ask him but finished his sentence. He said, "Ruth, I love you…" But he hesitated, and I blurted out, "*Jah*, I'll marry you. Will you marry me?" Timothy's light blue eyes stared in disbelief until his cheekbones rose, pushed up by a toothy smile. I soundly kissed him, so happy to find a man who loved me for who I was. *Finally*, in my late twenties, I was no longer an old *maidel*.

But I would have remained single if it wasn't for Timothy. *Ach*, I had a few court me, but they did not water me, open a dead seed, swelling it to life. *Nee*, they clamped me shut. *Jah*, they wanted to silence me. 'Spunky' is what some called me. Some plain old 'outspoken.' But Timothy adored this in me and miracle of miracles, still does!

Now there's a *boppli* growing inside and I can't wait to behold this young one. I do fear though that someone in our *Gmay* will find out I went to the Glory Barn to be prayed over, concerned I was too old to get pregnant. I snuck out with some local Mennonites who attend these meetings quite frequently. Only my sweet best friend knew, along with her husband-to-be.

Lena, my kindred spirit friend, looked so pretty in her green wedding dress, something forbidden back in our old *Gmay* in New York. It pained me that her sister snubbed her, not even sending a wedding card. Lena knew her mind well now, having had such heartache in life, now a fresh start with a new husband. Jacob loved not only Lena, but her two *wee* ones, even though they were from her first marriage to a brute of a man.

Ach, this love-filled union on Valentine's Day was restoring my dear friend. When Jacob wanted Groundhog Day to be their wedding day, Lena said they best not provoke her sister any further. I still laugh, and so do many in my church district, that Lena's sister thought the Amish were so liberal here in Pennsylvania that they worshiped a groundhog. Worshiped money made off all the *wunderbar* fun activities on Groundhog Day, selling pies, crafts and whatnot alongside Outsiders. Back in New York, we weren't allowed to even have a close English friend, but here we're allowed. Lena's sister declared it to be sinful.

Lena's big eyes met mine, sparkling with hope. *Ach, their vows were made? I wasn't even listening.* Was this me being pregnant? Or was it that all Amish said the same words during their five-minute-long vows, not like the Mennonite wedding I witnessed? *Ach, so romantic.* Why I keep thinking of the Mennonites when Timothy and I agreed to be committed to the Old Order Amish is a mystery. I was content in Pennsylvania. I could have a knitting circle in my new home and no one reprimanded me for talking about scripture. There was a mighty thirst among the People. And I planned, in my own small way, to water seeds in hearts the Lord brought my way. We all need to grow.

~*~

The intimate wedding with only thirty guests allowed time for everyone to talk. Lena embraced me tight and I heard a sob escape. I held her at arm's length and studied her. Her moist blue-green eyes were enhanced by the hunter green dress. "Happy, *jah*?"

"Ruth, can a woman be this happy?" Lena swiped a runaway tear.

I knew what she was thinking. Her late husband was all sunshine and roses until they got behind closed doors. "Lena, you can trust Jacob. There is no fear in love."

"You're right," she said. "It's a miracle the way he loves my *kinner*. Did you see him hold the *boppli* yesterday? Rocked her in the new hickory rocker you bought us."

"Well, he was taking a break from moving everything in your house right next door to mine," I chimed. "Now I'm the one who's too happy. I was so afraid you'd go back to New York."

Lena pressed an index finger to her lips. "Jacob's *daed* is right behind you."

Me and my mouth! I took Lena by the hand and asked her to close her eyes as I led her into the huge farmhouse kitchen. We meandered through tables set real pretty with white tablecloths. The red velvet cake that her aunt and I labored over half the night was hidden on the *eck* table under a box flipped upside-down. I slowly lifted the white pastry carton and told Lena to open her eyes.

She held her chest. "So many white roses!"

Knowing how much Lena yearned to grow climbing roses, it was fitting. The strict sect in New York where we both migrated from did not allow flowers to be planted because it showed pride. We were to be content to see wildflowers in the fields, but Lena had a dream of having a so-called *Englisher* looking yard, grass cut and even a trellis for climbing roses. "I didn't make the flowers, Lena. I must confess, Sarah did."

Lena looked past me and cowered. "They're not coming, are they?"

"*Nee*. Stephen and Sarah are shunned. Your aunt wanted a separate table and invite them, but when we got word that your in-laws were coming from New York, we didn't want to upset them any further. Remember, they don't believe in befriending anyone not Amish. No trusted *English* friends, let alone Ex-Amish."

"Well, Jacob wants to show his parents around these parts and mention land prices being so low." She winked. "Just like you did."

"So, he hopes his parents will move here? They have that huge dairy farm in Falcon Hill."

Lena twisted her white prayer *kapp* ribbons. "Sometimes I still feel selfish, taking Jacob away from the big King clan."

I took her thin hands. "You're worth it. Never doubt it that Jacob's happiest when you're being cherished." I leaned in to whisper. "I looked up the word 'cherish' in the Bible Dictionary and it means to warm up, like two birds huddled together."

Lena backed away. "Don't tease me."

Tease her? Fear was in her eyes. And again, I opened my mouth too wide. Lena was thinking of her wedding night. Fearful that Jacob would be like her first husband who tempted me on more than one occasion to hit him in the head with a frying pan. Seeing Lena bruised and all the excuses she made. *I fell. I'm so clumsy.* "I'm sorry, Lena. You'll see. Jacob will cover you, protect you under his feathers."

"You're right." Lena straightened and smoothed her white apron. "God has not given me a spirit of fear but of love. And I see God's love in Jacob," she said, her cheeks reddening. "I fret too much over the past."

Fear. That same old emotion haunted Lena even on the best of days. "I'm sure there're so many feelings running through you with living away from your aunt and uncle at your new place."

"I'm like their *dochder.* I think Aunt Naomi cried during the ceremony. Did you see her crying?"

"*Jah.* Tears of joy. Uncle Micah, too."

"Did I hear my name?" Aunt Naomi pealed out as she entered the kitchen. "Lena, do you like the cake?" She slipped an arm around her niece. "Red velvet cake, like you wanted."

Lena hugged her. "Ruth didn't say it was red velvet. *Danki.*"

"Sarah made the roses, but she didn't charge us, so there was no exchange of money with any Ex-Amish." Aunt Naomi embraced Lena, holding back tears.

"Lena embraced her. "*Danki* for the cake and everything. It's just what I wanted. Just wish…well, I'm glad I have you and Uncle Micah here."

This estrangement with her sister was something that made Lena like a pendulum clock, her emotions swinging back and forth. And once again I had to ask the Lord to forgive me for my anger towards Becky and her Pharisaical husband. Calling the bronze statue of Punxsutawney Phil outside the library an idol, comparing it to the golden calf worshiped in the Old Testament, had sent them packing. On Christmas Day, of all things, and demanded Lena return with them, as if she had no choice in the matter.

I was so proud of her for reasoning with them, not accepting the *Ordnung*, our rules for living that were too strict. Lena explained many Bible verses, but Becky just defended rules we'd grown up with. Thinking on it now, I was glad I received a warning for acting like an Evangelical Bible thumper, because I'd never have come to this place, The Secret Garden B&B, a haven of rest created by Aunt Naomi and Uncle Micah. And it was only two miles from our new farm.

~*~

After a hearty meal, we mingled as Lena and Jacob held hands across the little *eck* table in the corner. At times like this I wished I could use a camera. Lena was feeling ever so warm and tended to by Jacob, he was what I called him, 'pure sunshine.'

Feeling the *boppli* flutter a bit, I decided to get off my feet, so I headed back into the parlor, the pretty room where the ceremony was held. But as I drew near I heard Samuel King's voice and it didn't sound right as rain at all. I turned to head into the living room, but not before I heard him tell his wife he'd bring Jacob to his senses. *He'll never give up his inheritance.*

I stopped and leaned against the wall to hear more, my heart pounding. His wife, the dear woman, said it wasn't right to withhold money or try to stop God's plan. She loved the area and found the Amish people very kind, not so nervous and rigid. I expected this to ruffle Samuel King's feathers, but he grew quiet and admitted he was afraid. Afraid of losing his son to such a lenient Amish group. At this, I decided to enter the room and enlighten them. "So nice to see *yinz* could *git dahn* to the wedding."

They stared and squinted as if I was speaking a foreign language. Were they snubbing me, a worldly woman with a warning? "*Djew* get a root beer *pop* yet? I can *git yinz* one."

Martha King started to snicker. "I understood root beer, but that's all. People talk a little bit Dutch here, but it's not real Dutch."

I threw up my hands. "I'm sorry. It's called Pittsburghese. So many European immigrants settled in Pittsburgh and many of their words stuck. You hear some German, *jah*?"

"*Jah*," Samuel said gruffly, avoiding any eye contact.

"Samuel, I have to confess I overheard *yinz*, I mean you two talking about the Amish here being liberal."

He pulled at his shaggy beard and groaned.

"Well, some Amish thought it was too strict and became Mennonite. We all have our differences, but don't you think as Christians we need to see what we have in common? What unity we have?"

"*Jah*, I agree," Martha said, bobbing her head.

"Looks like rules are being bent a bit too much lately," Samuel stated with an air of superiority.

Learn from the dog, he wags his tail and not his tongue, I wanted to blurt. I'd never seen Samuel act so high and mighty. Is this why Jacob loved it here in Punxsy? "Your son has a *gut* head on his shoulders and decided to live here for *gut* reasons."

"Because of Lena. The man leads, not the woman."

I plunged my fists into my hips. He wanted to fight. Was I up to it? I shot up a prayer for help. "Samuel, Lena was willing to go back and live in Falcon Hill. She'd do anything for Jacob. As her best friend, I can tell you that she struggles with him not being happy away from his family."

"Really?" Martha asked, her fondness for Lena evident. "Samuel, it's like you said. You'll miss Jacob. A kinder son a *mamm* or *daed* could ever want."

Samuel looked down and pursed his lips. "He doesn't like farming. We're supposed to work the land. It's in the Bible."

"Jesus was a carpenter," I said humbly. "Jesus wasn't a farmer."

Samuel slowly cocked his head up like a tired rooster and frowned. "Jacob wants to be a carpenter…"

A sigh of relief blew out of me and Martha tried to squelch laughter but failed. "She's right, Samuel. Jesus was a carpenter. And who whittled wood since he was a *kinner*?"

"Jacob," Samuel admitted, shaking his head.

I knew what he was thinking. He'd been living in a box his whole life and it was high time to think outside of it. Did he need more help? "Paul was a tentmaker; some disciples were fishermen. More water on the earth then land. Why don't the Amish fish for a living? I really do ponder that."

Samuel gingerly sat on the sofa. He stared, thunderstruck, at the roaring fire. Martha pat his shoulder and gazed into the fire as well. Just when I was ready to try to hang up my teaching, preaching *kapp*, I saw the effect of the spoken word. I knew other Amish in our old *Gmay* who needed to hear the truth. The truth sets us free, after all. After we were settled in, I'd write Becky. Maybe plant a seed of hope? She should have been here for her sister's wedding.

Chapter 2

In my big old farmhouse we took possession of a month ago, I sat in wonder at the liberty I had to decorate. The dear folks from the *Gmay* came and slathered the walls in mint green paint. No stark white walls, but color. The honey oak kitchen cabinets were shiny enough for me to see my reflection and of all things, locals suggested a cement countertop. I thought it outlandish, but it was smooth as a river stone. Crews were in and out right quick doing many repairs; we got the farm cheap due to neglect. An elderly Amish couple had refused to live in a *dawdyhaus* behind their *dochder*, and they could not keep up.

While Timothy wanted to raise black angus beef cows, the former owners left sheep. Sheep to keep the grass down. Timothy said we could make a profit from the meat. Never did I hear of anyone eating mutton, but I suppose the English do and word had it that there was a real demand for legs of lamb for Passover. Someone at *Gmay* said that Pittsburgh had one of the largest population of Orthodox Jews who bought it for their special holiday.

When I raked my fingers through one, the yarn craving came on me. Yarn I could spin from the wool if Timothy would take my hints. Which he hadn't yet. I'd have to have Lena put a bug in his ear about getting me a spinning wheel. A woman in Smicksburg, only ten miles south, taught spinning classes and, well, there was just something about the feel of fiber of any kind between my fingers that calmed my soul.

I saw a figure through the morning mist and realized it was Lena. *Ach, Lord, I hope her wedding night didn't bring back Samson from the dead in her memories.* Lena's hasty walk made me think that not all had gone well. I met her at the door and she ran into my arms.

"He's *wunderbar gut* to me."

I sighed and then let out nervous laughter. "I was anxious on my wedding night, too."

"Samson didn't intrude upon my thoughts. *Nee,* just the opposite." She covered her crimson cheeks. "I wish all women knew what it's like to be truly loved, not just be used like Samson did me."

My friend said this without that twitch in her eyelid when speaking of her first husband. "I can tell love heals all, *jah*? Real love?"

"*Jah*. He gives us beauty for ashes, like you say."

"It's God's promise to you and me. We sure did have our ashes up there in New York," I groaned, still unsettled by Samuel King's aloofness.

"They're not all ashes up there in Falcon Hill. I had the oddest talk with my new mother-in-law yesterday. They said something other than farming could be God's will. Strange talk from folks back in our neck of the woods."

I poured Lena a cup of coffee and motioned for her to take a seat at my long oak table. "I talked with them about Jesus being a carpenter and they might have still been in shock. We never thought of that, did we?"

Lena snickered. "*Danki* for your help. I do feel for them, though. They'll miss Jacob and sometimes I wonder…"

"Don't be double-minded. You and Jacob both decided to settle here. I thought Jacob was shy, but it was

15

the old rules up in Falcon Hill choking the life out of him. Lena, do you realize how strict our Order was? We weren't even allowed to have the lanterns on our buggies hung evenly or it would show pride. That's *ferhoodled*."

Lena sipped her coffee and hovered over the mug. "My sister lives under such…"

"Bondage," I said. "They aren't free to do much. It's not natural."

"And the Mennonites think we have our bondages."

Lena was right. But I didn't feel enslaved like when we lived in New York. I tapped my heart. "I feel free in here. Freer to be myself."

Lena had perfect contentment oozing from her being. "I feel free in many ways. Free from my past and free to love Jacob."

This was *gut* news. *Gut* news indeed.

"Well, Jacob has the *kinner* and I best get back home. Ivy stopped by and brought a meal."

"What do you think of her?" I blurted.

"She's nice. Why?" Lena asked.

"Living right next door, I couldn't help but hear quarreling between Ivy and her youngest *dochder*. I hear she's leaving the Amish like her older sister. I think I'll stop over and chat with the girl."

Lena tilted her head. "Chat? You mean give her a Bible lesson?"

My brows shot up. "Me? Preach to someone? Never!"

~*~

I set two plates of roast beef, mashed potatoes, and green beans on the table and watched as Timothy licked his lips. I simply loved to serve my husband meals and was thankful the People had stocked our food pantry with canned goods, especially canned meats. "Timothy, you do love meat. Do you want to raise black angus cows to sell or eat?" I joked out of the blue.

"To sell." He rubbed his middle. "Am I gaining too much weight?"

"*Nee*, I didn't mean that."

"I am big boned and seem bigger than most."

I reached for his hand. "You're perfect for me."

We held hands as Timothy blessed the food, thanking God for not only this house but all that came with it, along with the sheep. He squeezed my hand, as was his custom. "You'll never believe what we're allowed to sell down here."

"Dolls with eyes?" I asked. "I can sew ragdolls with eyes."

"Well, *nee*. That wouldn't be right. And you can see all the snowmen don't have faces, *jah*? They do stick to Old Order ways."

"Then what can we sell that you're so excited about?"

His eyes danced. "Antiques. And we're allowed to go to garage sales."

I gasped. "You're joking. Go to an *Englisher's* house and see what they have to sell?"

"*Jah*. And there's an antique mall not too far from here. Yoder's Antique Mall that has one-hundred vendors. We can be one."

"A vendor? Come again?"

"We can rent out a space to sell things we collect."

I dabbed my lips with a napkin. "You've been to this antique mall?"

"*Jah*, I have. The neighbor next door stopped by when I was out walking the land and asked if I wanted to go."

I had two questions whirling in my head but the one in the forefront popped out first. "Did you see any antique spinning wheels over at the mall? They remind me of my *grossmammi*."

Timothy cupped my hand. "And you miss her? There's a train to Canada and we can afford it."

I smiled at how he loved me. "*Nee*, we write often."

"Are you sure? Thinking of her spinning wheel makes you sad."

"I'm not sad, just thinking…"

He let out a roar of a laugh. "Ruth Miller. Do you want a spinning wheel for your birthday?"

I set down my tea so my now jiggling, laughing body wouldn't spill it. "You know me too well!"

"I sure do. I saw how you got that yarn craving when petting our sheep. Maybe next month they'll have a spinning wheel over at Yoder's we can afford."

I chewed my lip, wondering if I should tell him about the woman in Smicksburg who sold spinning wheels. Not now. My second question was fresh in my ever-foggy mind. Pregnancy and a *gut* memory didn't go hand in hand for me. "What's Ivy's husband like?"

Timothy pursed his lips as if he'd bitten into a lemon. "Asa? He's nice and all, but he acts like some men up in Falcon Hill."

"What do you mean? Is he strict?"

"He talks down to his wife and *dochder*. Or maybe he's upset at them. Something's not right." Timothy took another heaping spoonful of potatoes and let out a 'yum.' "I married you for this cookin' and there isn't a day that goes by that I don't thank the Lord above."

"Timothy!"

"I'm joking."

"Tell me what you meant about Asa. You've got *gut* instincts about people. I wanted you to have a *gut* neighbor. We depend on each other more than others in the *Gmay*, as it should be."

"*Ach*, he's upset with his *dochder*." He clicked his fingers. "Too many new names to remember!"

"Serena. Her name is Serena."

"*Danki*. Anyhow, she's eighteen and not baptized. She talks too much to their other *dochder* who lives in Pittsburgh. To be honest, Asa seems rather down. Maybe he has the February blues."

I needed to know any information about this teenager I planned on helping. "Serena's a sweet girl at *Gmay*. Did Asa say why she's going fancy? Strict rules or something? I can enlighten her that the rules here are lenient."

Timothy's spoon almost entered his mouth. Almost. He stopped short. "Ruth, now, you've been given permission to share scripture here among the women, but don't go be a sidewalk preacher."

"A what?"

"An Evangelist!"

I straightened, not liking his tone. "Evangelist is one of your favorite characters in one of your favorite books, *jah*? *Pilgrim's Progress*. And he points the way and encourages. What's wrong with that? And it is one of the gifts of the Holy Ghost in the Bible."

The food on the spoon remained stationary. "Holy Ghost? You talk like someone who goes to the Glory Barns and preaches door to door. Wife, be careful."

"*Ach*, Timothy, you know I went to the Glory Barn and it's why I conceived."

"But only I know that."

"And Lena."

Timothy set the spoon back into the bowl. "Anyone else?"

"Jacob. Lena may have told Jacob."

Timothy ran his fingers through his fine blonde hair. "Ruth, if you get a warning here, where would we go?"

To the Mennonites, I wanted to say, but knew this would break Timothy's trust in me. We'd agreed and vowed to remain Old Order Amish under the Punxsutawney *Ordnung*. I would have to learn to be free inside. But I was never able to keep what was inside…inside!

~*~

February's weather in western Pennsylvania wasn't boring, that's for sure. Temperatures fluctuated by twenty or thirty degrees overnight. Today seemed spring-like at forty-three degrees as I hung out my wash on the line. To my surprise, I even saw a robin to boot. The air smelled like grass as all the snow melted, little rivulets streaming down the hill from the overflowing pond was calming to my nerves. And they needed calming since I was headed over to Ivy's place. With my house now in order, it was time to take some Friendship Bread over and a jar full of starter to pass along to another friend.

And I wanted to be Ivy's friend. From what I'd seen and heard over the past three days, especially at *Gmay* yesterday, was that Ivy needed to stand taller, not in a proud way. She seemed beaten down by life and I yearned for her to learn all that God said about her in the Bible. She was the apple of God's eye. I'd heard this saying, but to find it in the Bible surprised me to no end.

I let the air blow against my face, no need for an outer bonnet this glorious morning, and I wanted to swing my basket and skip, so happy I was, but then I thought of not only my *boppli*, but what other Amish would think of me acting like a schoolgirl. I still had this uncanny feeling that I'd get another warning from a bishop. Lena was right. I was too cozy with the Mennonites, but when you've yearned for a child as much as I did, I just had to take up their offer to go to the Glory Barn. I still believed God opened my womb.

Walking to Ivy's side door, I realized everything was as neat as could be. Was it the morning sun beaming on the doorknob or did it shine due to being polished? Ivy met me before I knocked, and her eyes landed on the basket; she covered her mouth to hide a smile.

"You didn't have to bring us over anything, Ruth."

"Friendship Bread and starter," I said, picking up the Mason jar full of batter. "You can pass this on to a friend."

"*Danki*. I haven't seen much Friendship Bread going around lately. I think I got a loaf a few years back."

"Isn't it an Amish custom everywhere?"

"I suppose. Maybe I just don't get picked much to get the starter." She scratched her chin as her face reddened. "Come to think of it, the last person to get this bread was when my Rose lived here."

As I followed Ivy in to her large kitchen, she appeared to droop like a rag doll. "Rose is my oldest *dochder* who left us for the English world. She lives in Pittsburgh."

I hung up my cape and when Ivy put cinnamon rolls on the table, I took the cue and sat on the bench. "How old is your *dochder* and when did she leave?" I asked, hoping not to be *nebby*.

When Ivy sat across from me, her eyes darted first to the utility room and then the living room. "Asa doesn't like me talking about Rose. He's made it clear to most everyone in our *Gmay*."

This woman was in deep sorrow over her *dochder* and her husband asked her to keep it to herself? "We carry each other's burdens, *jah*?"

Her hazel-gray eyes seemed to spark a bit. I found Ivy pretty for someone over fifty. Her salt and pepper hair didn't age her since her complexion was so clear and I couldn't find a wrinkle.

"Rose left five years ago. She wasn't baptized…"

"Then why doesn't she come visit? She's not shunned."

"Well, she took the baptismal classes and all, but Asa said she deceived us and he can't get over it."

I didn't want to prod any further. Something dreadful must have happened.

"My *dochder* decided not to be baptized when the man she was secretly courting left the Amish."

"And they ran off together?"

"*Nee*. He broke things off with Rose. But when we got word that Levi had become the town bad-boy, always down at the bar getting drunk, Rose was relieved they parted ways."

This was not going to be easy. I was going to have to pry this out of Ivy; she clearly wanted to tell me. "So, what did Rose do that was so deceitful?"

Ivy leaned forward and whispered, "She was seen talking to him in town. Rose confessed to trying to help him find the straight and narrow, but she was trying to lure him back with her charms. You know, charm is deceitful, like the Bible says."

I shook my head strong enough to feel my cheeks jiggle. "What?"

"You know that's in the Bible. Charm is *deceitful.* Rose didn't fear God if she was caught flirting with Levi."

I took a big bite of a cinnamon roll, dumbfounded. *Flirting? Deceitful?* Then God should have struck me dead when I was fifteen! "Has your *dochder* confessed to any *real* sin?"

"*Nee*, she said horrible things about my husband. Accused him of having no respect for women. But Rose's been causing trouble again; she's trying to lure our younger *dochder* to leave the Amish and live with her." Ivy's eyes misted. "Serena wants to leave, too."

Loud footsteps came from the living room and Asa made his presence known. Without even a hello to me, he set his jaw and crossed his arms. "Am I hearing talk about Rose in here?"

Ivy shot up and poured coffee into a mug. "Ruth's new here. Just getting acquainted." When she turned, her hand trembled, sending the hot liquid crashing to the floor. Asa ran to get towels and threw them on the puddle.

"Ivy, you're as clumsy as they come," he sputtered. "I told you these new wooden floors can't get soaked."

"I'm sorry, Asa. I *am* clumsy."

I slowly closed my eyes and prayed. This was Lena cowering under Samson's booming demands and insults all over again. *Well, Lord, you led me here for a reason.* "Your wife is nervous, not clumsy."

Asa peered up at me, his black shaggy eyebrows blocking his glare. "You don't live with her."

I tapped my foot, a nervous habit I'd developed over the years. After Asa wiped up any trace of coffee, he plunked down in his chair at the head of the table. A thought popped into my head, but did I dare share it? "Have you met Lena King?"

"*Jah*, sure. Why?" he asked.

"Do you think she's a happy woman?"

Asa smirked. "I don't gossip like the women. What's your point?"

"Jacob King is pure sunshine of a man. Lena was clumsy and so fearful of her first husband, and she couldn't make a decision to save her life. But she opened up like a morning glory around Jacob. Men are commanded to love their wives in the Bible for *gut* reasons."

"Are you saying I don't love my wife?" he grumbled.

"Who am I to judge? I just came over to bring Friendship Bread and starter. You know, to get neighbors…started on the right foot."

Asa clasped his hands. "I'm sorry. When I hear Ivy talking about Rose I know how upset she gets and…if you're going to come over to visit, talking about Rose is off limits. Maybe you didn't know."

I didn't want to be a meddling neighbor. That was not *gut*. "I'm sorry you're having such problems. I don't have *kinner* yet to know the heartache. If I can help your younger *dochder* find her footing in the Amish community, I'd be happy to talk to her."

Asa bat at the air. "All Serena says is the Amish are too strict."

"Well, I moved here for a reason. Timothy and I left the *Swartzentruber* Amish in New York. Serena has more freedoms than I ever had…"

"*Swartzentruber?*" Asa croaked. "They're odd."

"Would you talk to Serena?" Ivy bravely asked, straightening.

Asa said nothing, only stared at the floor.

"*Jah*, I'll talk to her."

Chapter 3

I feared that Asa would come over and complain to Timothy about his outspoken wife. But not a word, only Ivy sending Serena over with starter batter for Friendship Bread. Serena had that same milky smooth complexion as her *mamm*. With large dark brown eyes and a turned-up nose, I thought she was as cute as a button. When I asked her in, she shied away with a forced smile, giving me the excuse she was needed at home.

Today, the weather was so mild, Timothy and I headed to the antique mall to look at booth spaces, but we stopped at The Country Store first. I surveyed the vast variety of canned pie fillings and chose two cans of cherry and placed them in my basket.

"So good to see you, Ruth," Sarah squealed, giving me a hug.

I scanned the store to see if any Amish were in earshot. I couldn't be too friendly with this shunned

woman, but the store was empty except for Timothy.
"Sarah, so *wunderbar gut* to see you. How is Stephen?"

"Very *gut*. Look at my new dress." She turned around
and pointed to the darts in the waist of the blue calico
material. "Do they look okay? I'm not used to gathering
material, only straight lines like Amish clothes.

"You did a *gut* job. Did someone teach you how to
sew fancy?"

"*Jah*, other Mennonites. So many patterns to pick
from as long as they're modest." She touched her little
head covering that hid her bun. "I feel like my hair's too
exposed, but I'll get used to it. A lot less hair to deal
with."

"You cut your hair? How short is it?" I asked.

"It's to my shoulders. I admit, it was hard but
yesterday I decided if I'm going to be Mennonite, I
shouldn't be dressing Amish. I know how sacred they
view their distinct look."

"Well, you look good. How are things going at your
new church? I see the sign up in front of the red brick
building in town."

Sarah leaned close. "We're having a revival meeting
already. No need for a Glory Barn when we have a

building," she said with a chuckle. "It's in two weeks." She pulled out a flier from her purse. "Here, take a few fliers and spread the word."

As soon as she placed them in my hand, Timothy popped around the corner, his usual jovial face mighty downtrodden. He said hello to Sarah and ushered me away from her. "I'm done. Let's go."

I held up my list. "I have more things to get."

"Well, let's hurry up then. I, ah, need to check the sheep."

I cocked an eyebrow. "We're going to the antique mall after I'm done shopping. The sheep are fine."

Timothy led me to the back of the store, his large feet scraping loud as he went. "You are going to get a warning!"

"I can talk to Sarah, just not be too friendly." Timothy rarely got this flustered, his cheeks were cherry red. "And she needed to know if her dress was sewed right."

Timothy huffed. "I heard her say Glory Barn and she gave you papers. What's on them?"

I handed them over and to my utter shock, Timothy crunched them up in a ball. "I'll throw these in the stove when we get home. Good kindling."

I heard voices, so I knew the store was filling up. "You are embarrassing me. Now let's get over to the antique mall and I'll be praying I have strength to forgive you. You're treating me like a *kinner*. If you'd have given me time, I would have returned the fliers to Sarah."

"See, I told you. Amish women are ruled by their husbands."

Someone obviously wanted us to hear this. I spun around and saw Serena Coblenz with an *Englisher*. "Serena, he doesn't rule over me. We just had a misunderstanding."

Serena pointed to her friend. "I didn't say anything. Rose did."

"Rose? *Ach*, are you Rose Coblenz? Serena's sister?"

"Yes, I am," she said curtly.

Timothy spoke up. "We live next door to your parents."

Rose grew pale. "So, what do you think of my *daed*?"

"Well, he's…let me see. He knows what he wants. Real hard worker."

34

"Real bully you mean?" Rose spat out. "And he gets away with it because Amish men are all alike. Treat women like…" She bit her lower lip. "Amish men don't treat women right, let's just leave it at that."

Timothy put an arm around me. "This woman's happiness and wellbeing is more important to me than my own. I really mean that. We rarely have a cross word between us. I just got all riled up because Ruth got a warning where we used to live, and…"

Both girls' eyes widened.

"What did you do?" Serena asked.

"We came from the strictest Amish Order that there is. *Swartzentruber* Amish. Between us, lots of men acted superior to women. I decided in my early twenties I'd never marry, being controlled by a man. That's all they wanted when I courted. They tried to hush my outgoing personality." I wrapped an arm around Timothy. "But then I met this man and got married when I was twenty-eight."

The girls were speechless. I looked to Timothy to see if I'd said anything wrong. He was wearing the biggest grin, as if to say, 'That's my Ruth.' I wanted desperately to ask Rose to visit me, but I knew the wishes of the parents and apparently the *Gmay*. But I could see Rose was a hurting young woman.

"Where are you girls headed?" Timothy asked.

"I meet my sister here when I take her to Pittsburgh," Rose informed. "I'm not allowed to drive up to the house."

"Why don't we go get some pie somewhere and talk?" I asked. "Want to get to know Ivy and Asa 's *kinner*."

Rose looked away, her wispy shoulder-length dark hair fluttering out. "No thanks. Let's go Serena."

"*Danki*, but my sister wants to get on the road," Serena said apologetically. "I'll come over and visit you in a week."

"Bye now," Timothy said. He whispered in my ear. "She's looking at colleges in Pittsburgh. Asa is ready to throw her out."

"Throw her out? She's not baptized. Poor thing. She's like a stray cat, not secure in a home." My heart yearned to help this beautiful young girl. *Lord, use me as you see fit.*

~*~

That night I stood staring into my China closet drawer, admiring all my pretty stationery. I wanted to write on plain white paper in black marker "*BECKY, WRITE TO YOUR SISTER!*" I chose the prettiest paper though, the green paper with the blue forget-me-not flower border, and sat at my table to write.

Becky,

How are things up in Falcon Hill? How are your boys? I'm sure your busy not only with them, but also being pregnant. I find it exhausting most days.

I got a circle letter from my folks up in Canada and thought I'd start one with you. Enclosed is a letter telling about my latest adventures here in Pennsylvania. How about you write a letter to add and send it to someone in your Gmay and note that the last person to receive all the letters be Lena. That way she'll not miss her family and friends back in New York so much.

God bless you,

Ruth

I'd never started a circle letter. *Lord, forgive me.*

~*~

As the week continued, the weather dove to near zero degrees and ice filmed the roads. There were a few buggy mishaps among the People, but no one was hurt.

37

All week I thought of Serena, praying that somehow God would throw up a roadblock. Serena was leaving the Amish because of her *daed*, it was obvious. As I wrapped up three warm bread loaves and placed in my basket, I heard the door squeak open and there was Lena. She had that scared but brave look on her face. What we planned to do would be hard on her. "Are you sure you can do this?"

"*Jah.* And we timed it right. Just before the noon meal."

"And only Ivy and Asa are home. I saw Asa walk back into the house from his buggy repair shop." I grabbed my wraps and looped my arm through Lena's. "*Gut* to see you. Is little Eli feeling better?"

"*Jah*, just a cold. Was tempted to go over to Stephen's clinic, though. He wouldn't charge, and I didn't want to take advantage."

We steadied each other as we stepped down onto the icy road. "So, who saw Eli?"

"We hired a driver and took him to Reed Byler, an herbalist in Smicksburg."

"Smicksburg! I want to go there and look at a spinning wheel. There's a trusted English friend who owns a yarn shop and sells spinning wheels for a *gut* price."

Lena tightened her grip. "Ruth, we shouldn't be here on this ice. You're pregnant."

"I can ice skate pretty *gut*. Never fell. And we're almost there. Getting back to your Eli. You shouldn't feel bad taking him to Stephen. Drivers cost money."

"It was Jacob's decision," Lena said with a grin. "I think he favored the herbalist since *Grossmammi* King was so *gut* at home remedies and whatnot."

"And they were so close, he must be grieving still. Have any of the Kings written back?" I asked as we made our way around the sidewalk and rapped on the door.

"Nothing from either side. Have you gotten any letters from Falcon Hill?"

"*Nee.* I think they're glad to get rid of me, such an outspoken woman."

Ivy opened the door and gawked, stunned. "*Ach*, I can cook. No need for help."

I eyed Lena, not knowing what to say, poking her behind my cape to say something. "I want to repay you for all you did to help us move in."

Ivy sighed in relief. "Some may think I can't cook with Serena gone all week. Come in."

I looked for Asa to be at the head of the table, but no Asa. Well, it wasn't noon just yet.

. "Asa and I aren't hungry today. I'm sure the whole *Gmay* knows Serena is looking at colleges in Pittsburgh…"

"And you don't have an appetite?" I asked, truly concerned.

"We're fasting. Only bread and coffee."

"And we brought eight-grain bread!" I quipped. "It's mighty filling."

Ivy motioned for us to take a seat at her table with a broad smile. "That would make a nice change. We've been eating that awful store bought white bread now. I thought I baked enough for the week, but Asa is hungry for sure."

Ivy poured two cups of coffee from her speckle ware coffee pot and soon had a loaf of bread cut and we were all relishing the taste of my bread, minus any butter. "Is there something we can be praying about? Fasting is powerful."

"Powerful?" Ivy questioned. "We're fasting to be humble enough that God hears our prayers."

I started to speak, wanting to tell her God hears her prayers all the time, but Lena pinched my arm and took over the conversation. "I take it that you're praying for your *dochder* wanting to go to college, *jah?*"

I could no longer be silent. "Ivy, truth be told, I'm praying God will do something to stop Serena from leaving."

Ivy frowned. "We pray for God's will and accept it whatever happens."

As usual, I wanted to quote scripture about the power of prayer and bold faith, but I'd promised to let Lena steer the conversation. Our plan was that Asa hear her story and how much healing she found in Jacob. With Asa not here, maybe Lena could help Ivy.

"Ruth and I have said a similar prayer. We haven't heard from the People in New York. They think we're liberal Amish. The pain of the estrangement with my sister is awful. When I see Jacob too busy reading a book, I know it's to get his mind off his folks."

"I'm sorry to hear that," Ivy said, real heartfelt. "I know when Rose left, it was hard to get up in the morning, my sadness made me so tired. And now Serena…"

Lena reached across the table and took Ivy's hand. "I've known pain. If you ever want to talk."

"*Ach*, how silly of me to go on when you lost your first husband. That's a deeper pain."

Lena forced a smile. "You don't know me yet, so don't take this the wrong way. When a husband treats his wife right, it's natural to return the love. Samson was abusive to me and I cried more over the loss of the animals in the barn fire than him."

Ivy looked over at me in astonishment. "So, all Ruth told us is true?"

"Whatever Ruth says is true," Lena corrected.

"I didn't mean it like that," Ivy confessed. "It's just so hard to believe a woman would not grieve her husband's death."

"Lena's husband was a brute," I said, biting my tongue, wanting to ask if she'd be grieved if Asa passed away.

"My Asa has been accused of being a brute by Rose," Ivy said, her chin starting to quiver. "I don't see why she'd say that. He works hard to put this roof over our head. He was patient with Rose in my opinion."

"Why can't anyone talk to Rose?" Lena asked. "I've heard it at *Gmay*. Rose wasn't baptized, so she's not shunned."

Ivy's face turned to stone. "Rumors."

"Rumors about what?" Lena pressed. "Rose's your *dochder*. Why would you care so much about what others think?"

Ivy parted her lips, but nothing came out, only a tear ran down her cheek.

"Can we help you?" Lena wanted to know. "One thing I can be thankful for concerning my marriage is that the trial gave me a bigger heart and understanding for depressed women."

"Depressed?" Ivy swiped a tear. "This fast is making me emotional. I must lack Vitamin B."

As Lena continued to try to sooth Ivy, my mind was stuck on Rose calling her father a brute. And the more I dug around at *Gmay*, it was Asa who put it into folk's minds that Rose was trouble, someone who could bring bad influences among the People. Maybe I should be praying that Serena does find a college and live away from an abusive father. Lord knows he set the hairs up straight on the back of my neck. But how could a man be changed? Well, nothing is impossible with God…

Chapter 4

The afternoon sun melted the ice and Lena and I took the buggy over to visit Aunt Naomi. I had a few books to drop off at the library: mysteries. Were these books making my imagination soar a bit too high? I had a dream Asa committed a hideous crime…

As Lena caught up with her aunt, I stretched my legs out on the little daybed that was kept in the large kitchen. Memories of Lena resting here, bedridden to keep her *boppli*, although born a month early, flew through me.

"*Ach*, she's as right as rain is what!" Aunt Naomi yelled.

I knew Lena was bringing up Rose. "So, Aunt Naomi, what do you think of Asa? Is he another Samson?"

"Well, we can't judge. No two people are alike. All I know is Ivy looked younger when they moved here from

Montana. She was pregnant with Rose, though, so she might have had that pregnancy glow."

"Do they have kin here?" I asked.

"Word has it, they have some out in Lancaster. But their driver stopped here, and they got to looking at the newspaper and Ivy said they couldn't believe how cheap land was. They stayed a few nights and decided to settle here."

So, they'd lived here for over twenty years since Rose is in her twenties, I pondered. "Do the girls know their *bruder* out in Montana?"

"*Nee*, not much," Aunt Naomi said, with a growing smile on her face. "The girls think of me as an aunt. I guess I'm an aunt to a lot of people, even if by adoption."

She pat my hand and I felt loved. "*Danki*. It means a lot to me to feel like family." Memories of staying here in this B&B while deciding to move to Pennsylvania flooded me. I'd never felt so at home anywhere. "Aunt Naomi, maybe Serena can live with you! If she doesn't go to college, that is. She's miserable living with her parents."

"I'd love that, but I doubt Asa and Ivy would let her."

"She's eighteen," Lena said. "If she's still in *Rumspringa*, she could choose to live here."

I got so excited I clapped my hands. "I think we have a plan. I never thought being next door neighbors to that man could vex me so much. He yells at Serena something awful. And then it's so odd. Ivy bickers with the poor girl, seeming to take her husband's side. She acts so thankful he provides for them, as if they're pets."

Lena bellowed out a laugh. "You say the oddest things."

I cupped my mouth. "I suppose I do."

~*~

It being an off Sunday, with no church service, Timothy and I put our feet up to rest for the day. Of course, folks would stop by to say hello, but we were both bushed. Farming was indeed done by the sweat of the brow. But the more I was around the sheep, I yearned to shave them and spin their wool. My birthday was March eighth, only one week away, and Timothy seemed to forget anything about a spinning wheel. I hoped the book I was reading on spinning would throw my husband a hint.

47

But the more I read about sheep my fingers yearned to hold yarn, so I pitched the book and grabbed my knitting project always within arm's reach. The *boppli* sweater half done was on the kitchen table when I cooked; I'd take a break and get a few rows done.

A knock on our front door startled me. "Who uses the front door?"

Timothy tapped my hand. "I'll get it. Your ankles are swollen."

"They are? Or am I putting on weight everywhere?"

He lowered his head and smiled. "You're perfect for me."

Ach, it's what I said to him when I gave him a little hint he needed to stop eating the entire tray of cookies or whoopie pies. I baked when he went to the antique mall with Jacob the other day, so I'd have a treat to eat. *Is it possible my boppli has a sweet tooth?* I mused.

When I saw Serena and Rose come in the front door, I gasped. "Girls! You came over to visit! How was your week in Pittsburgh?"

The girls took each other's hands without a reply. "We have something to ask you," Rose said, rather gravely.

"Anything," Timothy said. "How can we help you?"

"Can Serena live with you?" Rose put a protective arm around her sister. "She just got kicked out."

"What?" I balked. "What happened?"

Timothy urged them to take off their wraps and led them to the settee near me. *This is pitiful,* I wanted to scream, but breathed evenly, knowing it said somewhere in Proverbs that there's two sides to a coin. Best listen to their side before going over and giving Asa a piece of my mind.

It was obvious Serena had been crying, but she sneezed and acted like she had a cold. "Aunt Naomi said I could live with her, but my parents said they weren't allowed to have Ex-Amish live there anymore."

"You are not Ex-Amish, Serena," I said. "Aunt Naomi and Uncle Micah won't get in trouble. But tell us first, what happened that you got kicked out?"

"I talk to Rose!" Serena exclaimed.

I eyed Rose as if she were on trial. What did this girl do to have so many Amish not want to talk about her? "Rose, do you need to make a confession? Why are the People not supposed to talk to you?"

49

Rose was undaunted. "I became an Evangelical Christian when I was on *Rumspringa*."

At this, Timothy went into a coughing fit. He slapped his chest a few times, as he doubled over. When all else failed, he ran into the kitchen to get a glass of water.

Rose's brows arched. "I upset him, saying Evangelical, didn't I?"

I nodded. "He calls me one. I love my Bible and talk about it a lot."

"Really? I teach small group Bible studies at Pitt. Well, at least I did when I went to college there. It's where I found Jesus."

Timothy returned to the living room, slumped in his rocker, and stared at Rose. "Amish don't take kindly to those who show pride."

"I know what you mean," Rose said. "Amish don't talk about their faith, they show it. I don't agree with their rules."

Rules. This was why we left Falcon Hill. Too many rules. "Well, I talk about what I'm learning in the Bible, not even intending to preach; it comes out naturally. Like at the quilting frolic this past week, we all got into a discussion about the Proverbs 31 Woman. Many of us feel inferior to her and we talked about it."

"That's what Rose does," Serena defended, "but my *daed* says she's too preachy and goes to a wild church. They have guitars and drums." Serena's pretty face lifted. "We went to the service last night and it was awesome."

"Drums and guitars in church?" I gasped.

Rose put an authoritative arm up to hush us all. "It's not my church or what I believe that's the problem. The truth is, my *daed* and I have clashed since I was born. It's like he hates me, and I don't know why. It's not natural."

My Timothy turned to putty. "Aw, I'm sure he loves you deep down. A girl, or should I say woman, like you would make her *daed* proud in a *gut* way."

"Woman for sure," I said. "You're only eight years younger than me, being twenty-two?"

She nodded. "I can make it on my own. It's Serena I'm worried about. She's only eighteen."

I had to ask Rose about what her parents accused her of. "This has nothing to do with a rowdy worldly man named Levi, does it? Rose, tell us the truth. I confess I asked about why we weren't supposed to talk to you and it all came down to this Levi."

"It's some kind of cover-up," Serena hissed. "If Rose was talking to him, it was to help him out."

Well this put me in my place but fast. "So, Rose, you're not taking Serena to wild parties on college campuses?"

"No, only wild churches," Rose said with a grin. "I think Serena and I will go talk to Aunt Naomi, if you're sure she won't get in trouble. She has a spare room."

"She can stay right here," Timothy said. "Ruth's pregnant and we could use the help. She's not baking for me like she used to." He winked at Serena to pull a smile from her. "Rose, you're welcome to stay until you need to get back to school."

Rose's eyes mellowed. "Thank you but Aunt Naomi's like a *mamm* to us."

I loved Rose's boldness. *Ach*, maybe a bit too much. Aunt Naomi taking in Rose would be a bold statement. She was not harboring Ex-Amish, but her door was open to those who chose not to be Amish. Timothy insisted Serena stay with us so she could make amends with her parents being right next door, and she surprisingly agreed. My heart warmed. Did Serena feel at home at our place? Would she let me help her? Be like a *mamm* figure?

~*~

Anna, my midwife, said I was showing too much for my first trimester and my desire to see Doctor Stephen grew. Truth be told, I wanted one of those ultrasounds that Lena had, telling me if I carried a boy or girl…or both. *Jah*, I have lots of movement for just one *boppli*, but what would I know, this being my first?

As the dawn broke over the horizon, like clockwork, Lena knocked gently on my side door. We read a scripture daily and prayed together, recording our requests in a prayer journal. This was our little time together, needing each other.

Lena popped in, fresh as this second day of March. "I didn't even have to wear a cape, just this sweater. *Ach*, Ruth, the winters in New York were so harsh."

"*Jah*, they were. I think Aunt Naomi should advertise her B&B to Amish up north, even up to Canada, since it's balmy here."

Lena helped herself to a cup of coffee and plunked down in the rocker next to me. "It's wash day. I dread it, with all those diapers. But I can't pray them away, *jah*?"

"You could use disposable ones, like the English," I suggested. "They sell them at The Corner Store and I see the Mennonites using them."

After sipping her coffee, Lena let out a sigh of utter contentment. "Ruth, Jacob is everything I dreamt of in a husband. Watching the *kinner* in the morning so I can chat with you, well it's just the opposite of Samson, who kept me chained to the house. I love it so much here. So, I won't complain about cloth diapers or anything. But I do have a hankering for something."

"What's that?"

"To go to Smicksburg to the yarn shop everyone talks about. And I think Eli would like to see the alpaca farms, too. Since we can hire a driver and ride in a car, I feel like the world's opened up."

Smicksburg? Did Timothy have a plan to get me to the shop that sold spinning wheels? Was Lena in on the plan? "I'm ready to go when you are. This week, maybe?"

"Maybe. Need to check with Jacob. He's taking those carpenter classes from Moses Miller and brings home such *gut* work. All kinds of fancy carved wood. Sure do wish Becky would write so I can share all I'm learning about freedom."

I held up the pretty pink flowered prayer journal. "We pray most mornings for Becky to write back. How about we pray God's will? I do get frustrated with that sister of yours. Doesn't she care that she's hurting you by all her silence?" I opened the journal and scratched out 'Becky to write' and put in 'God's will for Becky.' "I'm your sister, *jah*?"

Lena nodded. "*Jah*, we are. And since we're sisters, tell me what's wrong. I can see right through you."

My mouth grew dry. "Where to start... Did you hear that Serena is living with us?"

"*Jah*, Ivy came over crying. I feel for her. Asa makes her life as miserable as Samson made mine. I see it, Ruth. Something isn't right with Asa; he's hiding something."

"I just think Asa's one grouchy, stubborn man. Timothy's upset, but said he'd spend time working on him." I put Ivy in the prayer journal and 'Thy will be done,' next to her name.

"Pray that Ivy will really know God's love, Ruth. I spoke up about Samson when fear left me, knowing God loved me."

"Okay. Is there a scripture we're going to pray?"

"*Jah*, I have it. Ephesians 3:19. That she'll be able to know the love of Christ that passes understanding, so she'll be filled with the fullness of God."

I took notes as Lena said this unbelievable prayer. "Know the fullness of God. Seems like something we'll only know in heaven, *jah*?"

"Well, it's in the Bible. Maybe it's supposed to mean as much as we can take in until we go to heaven." Lena eyed the clock. "Only have ten more minutes. Fifteen minutes is too short. Maybe we can have a longer time to pour over scripture at my house."

I glanced around my living room, dreams of this place filled with a home Bible study taking root, but I knew it was forbidden. "*Jah*, we can meet at your place some days. Do you want to pray this morning?"

Lena nodded and proceeded:

"Lord, thank you for Ruth and her friendship, it means the world to me. I lift up Becky, Bud, and the boys to you. I lift up her pregnancy that all goes well, and she'll tell me by letter if something's wrong. Lord, we were so close, and I feel a part of me is missing and I'm torn. I'm Jacob's wife and live here, but I do miss her. Make her write.

"And Lord, whatever is going on in Ivy's house, protect her and help her know Your love so fear will be gone, and she can speak up. Or, heal her heart from such a man as Asa, his words so cruel. I've come to really care for Ivy and hope you can help their family. Help Serena while she lives here, and Rose as she heads back to Pittsburgh.

"We ask all this in Jesus name.

"Amen."

"Amen." Poor Lena, she missed her ungrateful sister up in New York too much. But they only had each other when their parents died in a buggy accident when Lena was ten and Becky fifteen. And Samson still haunted her, seeing him in Asa.

"What's wrong, Ruth? Be honest."

"*Ach*, I just think Becky's unkind to you and it bothers me."

"What else? You're concerned about something much deeper."

My eyes bugged. "You can read me like a book! *Ach*, Lena, I want Stephen to do an ultrasound on my *boppli*. Anna said I'm big for my first trimester and I feel so much movement."

"Ruth, you've never been pregnant. It's normal to feel a flutter here and there."

"I don't trust Anna's judgment, plain and simple. She's not a medical person like Stephen."

Lena shot a stern look. "You're already hiding visiting the Glory Barn, want to have a Bible study, and now you want to get an ultrasound that costs money? We can't exchange money with Ex-Amish."

I shook my head. "Who said I was planning on having a Bible study here?"

Lena motioned around the room as she rose. "Too many chairs and benches in a circle for just you and Timothy."

"Serena's living here, too. And we get company."

Lena leaned over to give a swift hug. "Company where you can spread those seeds you plant… Evangeline."

"Evanga-what?"

"*Ach*, I'm reading a book Ivy gave me, *Uncle Tom's Cabin*. It's about slavery of all things. I suppose Ivy can relate to Uncle Tom. Anyhow, there's a character named Evangeline, called Eva for short. But it means a female evangelist."

I blinked in disbelief. "You really think Ivy's like a slave?"

"*Jah*, I do. Do not say a word to anyone, though. We're new here and used to men being too strict in Falcon Hill. I want to try to change Asa slowly. Well, I'm hoping our husbands can rub off on him." Lena ran towards the door. "Have a *gut* day...Evangeline!"

"You, too," I said with a chuckle. Who ever heard of a female evangelist?

Chapter 5

Later in the day, after I finished my wash, I was as wrung out as my new wringer washer. But with Serena's help, it was less of a trial. My back ached with the weight of my *bopplin*. I just knew I was carrying two *kinner*. Was this a *mamm's* instinct? Should I prepare for twins or go over and chat with Stephen when getting supplement samples?

Serena made the noon meal and we threw together a few leftovers for dinner, wash day being so grueling. Timothy was tired as well, farm work along with trying to partner with an *Englisher* to get enough antiques to rent a spot at Yoder's Antique Mall. He was running himself ragged, and I feared he'd catch the spring flu going around. Funny how locals called it spring already, while back up in Falcon Hill it wasn't spring until May. *Danki Lord we moved here!*

The three of us sat in the living room, Timothy reading stacks of books on sheep while I taught Serena how to cast on, the first step in learning to knit. But, there was a rap on the front door. Timothy got it as usual and Rose stepped in, followed by Ivy. I felt my stomach turn. Ivy probably wanted Serena to go home. And Rose was here to prevent it? "Rose, I thought you went back to Pittsburgh."

She smiled. "Stayed at the Secret B&B for a couple days to…talk to Aunt Naomi."

Ivy rolled her eyes, and then took a pie out of her basket and lifted it up for Timothy to sniff. "It's lemon custard pie. Want some?"

"*Jah*," I exclaimed, shocking myself. Was I ever full carrying these twins? "I'll get plates."

"You sit, and I'll get plates," Serena said. "I'm here to help you and need to earn my keep."

Ivy licked her lips. "Rose and I wanted to thank you both for taking in Serena."

Serena neared her sister and whispered something in Rose's ear, which appeared to make Rose grave. Such sorrow in one so young. Or was Rose like me, so independent, clashing with other men, not able to find a beau who'd love her for who she was? I'd add her to the prayer journal.

Ivy noticed the tension and smiled at Serena. "I'll be right next door," she encouraged.

I wanted to yell out, *Why can't she live with you? She's your own flesh and blood. Tell Asa to leave!* But I knew better. Serena would feel most unwelcome in my home if I did. "I really do need help and glad you can stay, Serena. Now, let's enjoy that pie!" I sounded too chipper and Timothy gave me that look as if to ask what's wrong. *Asa Coblenz was what was wrong.* This was absurd to have a daughter living next door, not welcome in her own house. I tried to think of something pleasant to say. "Ivy, when can we plant lettuce outside down here? I ache to start my kitchen garden."

"It's only March," Ivy said. "You can plant snow peas, kale and other hearty vegetables in April, but the last week in May is when we put in our plants. It's the one day out of the year Asa and I go to pick out flowers to plant around the old water pump."

"Which is pathetic," Rose groaned. "Wish I could take you to Pittsburgh with me."

Ivy's mouth gaped. "It's snippy remarks about your *daed* that give people reason to avoid you."

Rose held her peace, but she seemed like she wanted to explode; her eyes bulged as she wiped perspiration beads forming on her forehead. Why did Ivy defend such a man? Was Lena wrong about her assessment? Was Asa not like Samson at all? Was he just a worried man who had a wayward daughter who he feared would influence Serena?

"*Ach*, I almost forgot," Ivy said, digging into her apron pocket. "Two letters came to the wrong address."

I noticed one envelope had the logo of a spinning wheel. Was Timothy ordering one? Was it on its way? My heart leapt. But when I saw my letter to Falcon Hill with "RETURN TO SENDER" written on it, I wanted to scream. *Becky, you self-righteous hypocrite! Lena's too sweet to be treated like this!*

"Mail keeps coming in for Lena, too. The new rural route mailman needs to learn to read addresses right."

My face was ablaze with indignation. "*Ach*, I'm so upset. Lena's sister returned the circle letter I tried to start."

"I couldn't help but notice the bold letters," Ivy confessed. 'Poor Lena. But she has Jacob, *jah*? Happy with her second marriage? She told me her story."

"Me, too," Rose said, as bitter as if she just sucked on a lemon. "Jacob loves Lena; he treats her like an equal, like the Bible says to do. Husbands love your wives…or your prayers won't be answered. Sure don't think God hears my *daed's* prayers."

Ivy clamped a hand on Rose's shoulder. "I think it's time for you to go."

"I'll walk with *yinz* to Rose's car," I offered, wanting to plant some encouragement in Rose.

"I had to park it at Lena's so my *daed* wouldn't see it. He's so absurd."

"Rose!" Ivy yelled. "He's fed you and put a roof over your head. Be grateful."

"We do that for our sheep," I said evenly.

"*Jah*, there's more to love than providing food and shelter," Timothy said. "Rose, I'm sorry you don't feel like your *daed* loves you, but remember, you have a Heavenly Father who does."

Rose raised her hand. "Hallelujah for that. Thank you, Timothy. You'll make an awesome father."

"I hope so," Timothy said, opening his arms to embrace Rose.

I wanted to shake Ivy, tell her to wake up. Didn't she see her hurting daughter?

~*~

"Happy Birthday, sweetheart," Timothy chimed, moving his large hands away from my eyes.

An oak cradle sat on the kitchen floor. No spinning wheel, but something for the *boppli*. My heart plunged. How many times had I hinted at a spinning wheel?

"What do you think? Jacob made it. Learning carpentry mighty fast"

"So, it's from Jacob and Lena?"

He pivoted me around. "It's from me. You don't like it, do you? *Ach*, I'm not good at giving gifts."

His defeat couldn't stop me from assuring him it was a *wunderbar gut* cradle and a fine gift. I hugged him around the middle. "*Danki*, Timothy, but I think we'll need two cradles"

"*Ach*, Ruth, you still want to see Stephen, *jah*? Get an ultrasound?"

I nodded. "I just know there's two souls in my womb."

He kissed my forehead. "Lots of work to do. We can talk tonight."

"It's my birthday," I stated a bit too firmly, like a spoiled child. "We always spend the whole day together."

"I'll make it up to you, I promise. I got a ride to the antique mall to sign the papers for our booth."

"I'll come with you."

"There's no room."

"How do you know?"

"I just do."

"Well, I suppose that's that. Then I'll have the buggy and go somewhere with Lena."

"Have fun," he quipped as he near skipped out the door. How strange. It's as if he doesn't want to be around me, like he's hiding something.

Serena stood behind me, and when she spoke up I jumped. "Didn't see you there."

"What do you want me to do next? I can take the rugs out and beat them. Looks like the braided one upstairs has seen better days."

"I can't help you lift…"

"I can do it myself."

"Okay, then. I think I'll *redd* up around the house here and there, nothing too heavy. Feeling rather wrung out." I darted towards the stairs so Serena wouldn't see me sulk. Since I had no control over my birthday disappointment, straightening things up in drawers or whatnot made me believe some things were under control. I'd been wanting to write my family in Canada as well. Not even getting a birthday card, they might have forgotten I existed.

I decided to write a letter first, as it was therapeutic to get my thoughts out. I sure was glad Lena popped over for fifteen minutes to pray, or I may have unraveled.

Unravel. That's what yarn did. And a spinning wheel would spin it back together. How could Timothy be so daft! I searched for a pen but found none. Timothy had a nasty habit of underlining his books and taking my pens. Maybe Serena had one in her room. I walked down the hall to her little space to see if she had one on her desk, and there was one. And a cellphone. *Ach, could this day get any worse?*

I did what I only knew how to do. I went back to my bedroom, closed the door and got down on my knees and remained silent. This calmed me down and made me focus on God. I took in a deep breath and closed my eyes, but all I saw was the spinning wheel in the catalog and Serena's cellphone. *What to do, Lord? I need to accept disappointments as your appointments, jah? You're building character in me. And at least I can be assured that Timothy is a gut man who loves me, just a horrible gift giver. Like the time he went to the feed store to buy me fifty pounds of cracked corn so I could feed the birds. How romantic! Lord, while you're building character in me, can you develop a knack for gift giving in Timothy? He just doesn't pay attention to details!*

I heard a train. What? There wasn't a train nearby. What on earth. I rose to follow the sound which led me to Serena's room…to her desk, the cellphone lit up with the name *Rose*. I gulped and shot up a prayer as I heard pounding footsteps ascend the stairs. Serena ran into her room, but came to a halt when she saw me.

"That's Rose's ring. She loves trains."

"Excuse me? Serena, you are not allowed a cellphone, are you?" It just dawned on me that Serena was on *Rumspringa*. "Our *Ordnung* says only cellphones for business, but you must be on *Rumspringa*," I fumbled. "But did you have it at your parents' house?"

"*Nee*. My *daed* would have taken it. Rose bought it for me now that I live here."

"And you think we'll be lenient?"

She bobbed her head. "You're full of kindness here. I never realized how much tension there is over at my house. Can I keep the phone?"

"Well, as long as Bishop Dan is okay with it, then there's nothing to hide, *jah*?"

Serena plopped down beside me. "Please don't tell the bishop. It's my only link to Rose. What if she's in trouble in the city? She may need to call me."

"Really," I said flatly. "No 9-1-1 calls in the city? She has no friends? No church friends she can contact?"

Serena frowned, a tinge of anger about to erupt. "We only have each other. Rose is the only one who knows what it's like to come from such a family as ours." She clenched her fists and rolled her eyes. "I've never met anyone who lived in a house of horror before and was Amish."

"We all have our sin nature to deal with. No one's perfect. Serena, I don't mean to be harsh, but have you taken the log out of your eye to see clearly the speck in your parent's eyes?"

"I see plenty *gut*. My *daed* doesn't love my *mamm*. It's a pity since she's so pretty and he's not so *gut* looking. My *mamm* could have married someone else who would treat her better."

I let Serena vent. I knew what it was like to be eighteen and think I knew everything.

"One of these days, he's going to kill her."

My heart fluttered, stunned by these words. "Kill her?" The mysteries I'd been reading helped me find a real murderer. It was always the least suspected person. Asa got all riled up but calmed down. *Not the profile of a killer.* I shook my head. *No more mysteries!*

Serena's lips formed a thin pink line. "Not actually kill, but slowly suck the life out of *Mamm*. Treats Rose the same."

I studied Serena's face. She talked as if reliving a past horror, ever so fresh in her mind. With some difficulty, I knelt in front of Serena so we were eye level. "Let's tell Bishop Dan."

"*Nee!* Things will only get worse."

Now my fists were clenched. "Your *mamm* can live here, too."

Serena leaned her pretty head on my shoulder. "We both know there's no divorce allowed among the Amish. Please, can I keep the cellphone…in the barn, like businesses do?"

I wrapped an arm around this dear girl. "I suppose you could keep it out of the house. But don't trust in a phone call to help you and Rose. Look for the path across the roaring river."

"Like stones you step on to get across a creek?"

"Exactly. You catch on quick. For now, we'll just watch and pray, like the Bible says to do."

"Watch what?" Serena wanted to know.

"Watch your *daed's* behavior and watch out for your *mamm*."

Serena hugged me. "I'm so glad you're here. But I do wish somehow one of my *bruders* out in Montana would visit and talk sense to my *daed*. Only met one once, the oldest, and he seemed normal. *Daed* was the nicest I'd ever seen him. He hates womenfolk."

I tried to digest this new revelation. Timothy was generous, lending money to Lena when Samson drank away all their money. Would he be so kind as to buy a train ticket so one of the Coblenz boys could come out and help their sisters? It was getting near planting time, though, so I suspected not. And Timothy seemed so short on money lately. Didn't even have enough to buy me a spinning wheel? I clearly threw big hints, even cutting out a picture of it and putting it in his Bible. He probably just used it to underline something!

Chapter 6

Lena pressed an index finger into her lips to hide a smile. "Never thought I'd get a spinning wheel. Do you like it?"

It was honey oak colored, like my kitchen cabinets. This belonged in my living room, not Lena's! "I like it. Let's head back outside. And Lena, you got dirt on your lips. Don't lick."

Lena rubbed her mouth against her gardening apron as we headed back to her garden. "I'm a mess, *jah*? I keep thinking planting so early is a mistake, but snow peas and kale and other cold crops the locals say are safe if covered with this plastic." She picked up the end of the long clear sheet that would go over the arches Jacob made with pipes. "It's like a greenhouse."

"I've seen them around, but Timothy is…busy. I hinted at wanting to get seeds started inside, but he keeps telling me to keep my feet up. Lena, sometimes I think I'm having twins. Look at me! I'm huge for one *boppli*."

"Are not," Lena quipped. "You're barely showing. Not waddling around yet."

I stepped closer, so not even the robins building nests in nearby trees could hear. "I want an ultrasound; Stephen could do it."

"What? *Nee*, Ruth. Mine was done before I knew what was happening. Praise be I didn't have a miscarriage. But you're healthy and, well, ultrasounds cost money you don't have."

I didn't think it cost that much if Stephen had the equipment. Surely the clinic had something like that. I fixed my eyes on the cumulus clouds ahead, the vivid blue accentuating these puff balls in the sky. Puffy indeed, just like me!

"Ruth, please stay clear of shunned Amish. It is part of our vow. I don't like keeping it a secret you went to a Glory Barn meeting." She forced a smile. "It's your birthday, so we can't talk about anything disagreeable. Now, I have a present for you."

In the distance I saw Timothy returning home, his horse trotting rather fast. "The best birthday present is having you living right next door. Still pinch myself to see if I'm awake. How about you give it to me tomorrow during our little fifteen-minute prayer time."

"I can't…"

"Why not?"

Timothy pulled into Lena's driveway, waving at me to beat the band. He jumped out of the buggy, mischief on his face. *Jah*, that impish grin said he had a secret. "How's my birthday girl?"

"Fine. Why so happy?"

"Stopped by the auction house. We can afford cows!"

"I want Merino sheep for their wool."

"Who needs sheep when you can raise cows?"

Lena leaned over to gather her gardening tools. "Timothy, are you ready for that special cup of coffee we talked about?"

"*Jah*, sounds *gut*. Warm all day but getting nippy." He rubbed his hands together and then reached out for mine.

I wanted to spin around and head home. Why was Timothy being so pig headed about getting cows? I asked Lena if she needed help taking in anything to her garden shed, but she motioned for me to go on inside.

"Ruth, you don't look too chipper today. Something wrong?" He wrapped his arm around my shoulder, nearly pushing me towards Lena's side door.

"I saw Lena's spinning wheel. Real nice."

"Jacob got a *gut* price from the lady in Smicksburg. I hear there's more for sale, but with getting more cows…"

I clamped my eyes shut and prayed for the strength to not pity myself. "And Merino sheep."

Jacob was the picture of fatherhood, rocking Susan while keeping an eye on Eli in the living room. "Did you come over for coffee? *Now?*"

"Now," Timothy boomed.

Lena hugged me from behind. "Happy Birthday, Ruth!"

"*Jah*, happy birthday, Ruth," Jacob said.

From their behavior, I half expected the whole town to jump out from around the corner and yell "Surprise!" But not a peep. "Well, *danki*."

Timothy took my hands, while he shook with laughter. Lena uncovered a birthday cake she'd hid under cheesecloth. "We'll have this after dinner. Made you something special. A nice meal for just our two families."

Timothy cupped his mouth to whisper something in Jacob's ear, nodding in understanding, and then sprang up the stairs. What on earth? Now, Jacob was smirking, and Lena gave him that knowing look that she knew a secret. Loud pounding down the stairs as Timothy held a large box. He huffed when he got to the bottom. "Heavier than I thought, or my backs going out."

"Are you all right?" I asked.

He rushed to my side. "Do you like Lena's spinning wheel?"

"*Jah*, really nice."

He embraced me so hard, I could barely breathe. He let out a victory shout, saying he'd gotten me the same one. I flung my arms around his neck. "*Danki*, Timothy. What a jokester you are!"

"Did you really think I'd give you a cradle for your birthday when half of Punxsy knew you wanted a spinning wheel?" He released me and chuckled. "And a breeding pair of Merino sheep will be ready to pick up next week."

I squealed and hugged him with all my might. What did I ever do to deserve such a man?

~*~

79

Over the next week, Lena and I tried to get the calming rhythm of spinning down pat. We continued our fifteen-minute morning coffee prayer time as well, but Jacob was getting grief from Asa, proclaiming tending to *kinner* was for the women-folk. What a burden Asa was becoming. Lena's face contorted when relaying her progress in trying to help Ivy. And not much got Lena down in the mouth these days, feeling so nurtured in her new marriage.

Today Timothy and I were headed to the auction, and Asa invited himself. I don't know who I was more annoyed with, Asa or Timothy for telling him he could tag along. Timothy just could not say no, always wanting to help someone in need; Asa was in need. He needed church discipline, the way he ignored Serena and hammered down on Ivy. As for Rose, she wrote regularly to Serena, occasionally to me, asking if Lena was helping her *mamm* at all. I could only be truthful and say to pray. Ivy needed help.

"Are you ready to go?" Timothy asked, rubbing his hands together in glee. "I'm like a kid in a candy shop when it comes to auctions."

"We're only going to get baby chickens, *jah?*"

"Well, we'll see what they have to offer. May have more sheep." He winked, a grin pushing up apple cheeks.

"Lena and I are just beginners. Don't make fun," I protested. "We get frustrated because we need classes. Maybe go to Smicksburg to the lady you bought the spinning wheel from." I rubbed my protruding belly. "Bending over shouldn't be so hard on my back if I was carrying one *kinner*, but Timothy, I know there's two."

He pointed upwards. "Only God knows."

"And Stephen could do a Doppler monitor test real cheap. He could find two heartbeats."

Timothy let his eyelids close like shades. "Please, don't be so cozy with the Mennonites. We want peace here, *jah*? There's been no warning from Bishop Dan about you having some women folk over to knit so far…"

"But, Timothy, I can't help but share all God's doing. Serena says I help her with having such a man as Asa as a *daed*."

Timothy repositioned his straw hat on his head. "Do you pray for Asa?"

"I think you pray enough for both of us," I spat, covering my mouth in shock at the anger that just erupted. "I'm sorry. So sorry. I didn't mean it like that. He just makes me so nervous. I'm so afraid for Ivy. He's going to drive her mad."

Timothy put up fingers one at a time. "Your due date is in October, *jah*?"

"End of September, if it helps you," I quipped. "So, six and a half months left. If I go early like Lena did, only five more months of this emotional woman you have to live with."

He opened his arms and I flew into his embrace. How I loved this man. "I still think you need another cradle if I'm carrying twins. And wouldn't you want to know if I was?"

He squeezed me. "I want to be surprised."

I rested my head on his chest. "Does Asa have to go today? He unnerves me."

"*Jah*. I think I'm making some progress with him. Iron sharpens iron, and I believe some rough edges are coming off. He's been talking more about his life in Montana."

Lord, help me deal with that man today!

~*~

82

I sat between Timothy and Asa, feeling mighty uncomfortable. Asa complained like a leaky faucet. *Drip, drip, drip.* Had he nothing pleasant to say? "Asa, do you miss the big blue skies of Montana?" I asked, wondering if the cloud coverage over Pennsylvania bothered him.

"Always had my nose to the grindstone, making a living. No time to look up at the sky."

I clucked my tongue and Timothy put an arm around me, a warning to calm down. "What Ruth's saying is maybe you should look up at the sky from time to time. Ever watch the stars? I have a constellation chart and am a bit of an astronomer."

Asa's mouth gaped. "That's evil. Reading the stars is forbidden."

"*Nee*, that's astrology, telling the future by the stars. Astronomy is pure science."

"The heavens declare the glory of God," I added. "And it makes you realize how small you are compared to God. It shows me God is in control because he holds the universe together."

Asa cracked a knuckle. "I don't need preached at by a woman."

Timothy groaned. "She's not preaching, just sharing a Bible truth."

"If Ivy talked like that -"

Timothy and I ignored him when the pigs were being brought out. I loved pigs, not to eat but for a pet. The smartest animal of all, I had one for a pet as a *wee* one and watched eagerly as little piglets were brought out into the middle of the auction house. I looked across at the stadium benches, many pointing and *kinner* laughing, tugging at their parent's sleeves to buy one. *Englisher kinner*, not Amish. Amish *kinner* knew not to beg; and here I was wanting to beg Timothy to get me a piglet. "They sure are cute," I mumbled in his ear.

"Daisy's long gone, Ruth. You'll be having a *boppli* with no time to take care of a pig."

"We'd need two. They don't do well on their own. If we had two, I would only have to slop them. *Ach*, they're so cute." I wanted to squeal in delight, seeing their curly tails.

The sound of a chicken pierced my ear. It was Asa, clucking. What on earth? He jabbed over at Timothy's knee. "Hen pecked man is what you are. Ruth wants sheep, you get sheep. Now Ruth wants a pig. Going to give in?"

Timothy eyes glazed over. "Ruth is sitting right here. Don't be rude."

"Well, it's the truth. You spoil her, like Jacob does Lena."

I felt my anxiety level raising, my ears and neck getting hot. I started to do little prayers I'd learned when anxious. Rose wrote to me with a list of 'Breath Prayers.' Not anything mystical, but short little prayers to say when my mind went into a tailspin to be said with a deep breath. I closed my eyes and prayed, *'When I am afraid, I will trust you.' 'Not my will, but Yours.' 'Lord, have mercy.' 'Come Lord Jesus.'*

"What are you doing?" Asa asked. "The New Age meditation like Rose?"

"What? It's not New Age. I'm just praying with my eyes closed."

He chuckled. "Rose did that, silly girl. We Amish pray in silence, I could hear you."

"You could? Well, maybe I should have added, 'Lord, have mercy on Asa's soul!'"

He gawked and then slowly slithered close. I backed away, wondering why Timothy wasn't intervening.

"I know you went to a Glory Barn meeting. You and Lena best stay away from my wife or I'll tell Bishop Dan."

My throat constricted. Who let this out? Lena? Surely not. Maybe a Mennonite who was there. Sarah? Stephen? I wanted to cry until I heard Timothy bid on two little piglets. Asa clucked up a storm and being heavy on the nest I wanted to shove him down the bleachers, but slowly closed my eyes, trying to compose myself.

"Are you going to get her another sheep, too?" Asa hissed.

"Honey, do you want more sheep? They're coming up next."

"Jah, maybe one more, unless they have alpacas."

I knew what Timothy was doing. *Provoke one another to love and good works*, a Bible verse we were discussing. All the bickering with Asa left Timothy unsettled, so he talked to Bishop Dan about it. The bishop said sometimes we stir up or provoke those who know they need to change. He advised Timothy to get to know Asa all the more.

Dear Lord, give me strength!

Chapter 7

Unloading the wagon with two piglets in a feed bag, Timothy deciding not to get a sheep, I was glad this venture was over. Asa got three hens, all huddled together, awful fearful. Did they know their owner was a bully? *Ach, Lord forgive me. That man unnerves me to no end!* I needed to end this most unpleasant day on a better note. "Asa, want to come in and have coffee? I have a pound cake and you could sit and chat with Serena."

Asa jutted his chin. "Wayward girl."

I turned to hide my grimace. I caught Timothy's eye and he took over. "Ever see your sons in Montana? Miss them?"

He shoved his hands in his pockets. "Well, it's far. *Nee.*" He took his hens and mumbled a thank you for the ride and trudged out of the barn.

When he was out of earshot, I shook my head and raised my hands. "Thank God I waited until an old *maidel* to marry you. I believe Daniel Troyer would have treated me like Asa."

Timothy pet the piglet. "That man treats his horse better than people. I'm sorry I let him come along with us."

I scooped up the other piglet and it nudged its snout towards my face. "She wants to give me a kiss. So sweet. Well, dear husband, I need to get inside and make supper."

Timothy kissed my cheek. "Just put out sandwiches. I'm stuffed from the pulled pork over at the auction, and you look bushed."

I was tired. Carrying twins was exhausting, I wanted to say, but kept this to myself. Maybe it was wishful thinking, having *kinner* later in life, wanting to make up for lost time. As I headed towards the house, I noticed the oddest thing; a photograph on the barn floor. Picking it up, I was utterly shocked to see a picture of an Amish woman. I turned the photo over to see the name Rachel Coblenz. Rachel Coblenz? "Timothy, I think this fell out of Asa's pocket. Come see."

Timothy peered over my shoulder. "Rachel? Is that Asa's?"

"Does he keep it in his pocket?" I asked. "Did he just drop this?" I shifted. "And photography is forbidden."

Timothy placed a hand on my shoulder. "You don't think it's Serena's or Rose's?" He sighed audibly. "Maybe it's a relative who's Old Order Mennonite? They get their pictures taken."

Just then Serena emerged from the house to unpin the clothes on the line. "I hear squealing pigs. Did *yinz* get some?"

We nodded in slow motion.

"I know I shouldn't have left the clothes on the line since this morning. Was busy filling out college entrance forms."

"*Ach*, you didn't do anything wrong," I assured. "Come here, Serena." I searched the photo to see any resemblance to Serena or Rose but saw none. I handed the picture to Serena. "We just found this. Did you drop it out here? Says Rachel Coblenz on the back."

Batting her lashes to beat the band, Serena grew pale. "Never saw her face before."

"Whose face?"

"My *daed's* first wife's."

So, my intuition was right. Asa kept this photo like hidden treasure. Poor Ivy! Did she ever come across it? Surely she did if it fell out of Asa's pocket. Grief filled me. Asa treated Ivy like leftovers.

"What are you going to do with it?" Serena asked.

"We need to return it to your *daed*."

"You should tell Bishop Dan he keeps a photo in his pocket. It's about time he gets a warning for something other than…"

Timothy chimed in. "Now, we know the Bible says to settle something one on one, humbly, to try to win back a brother."

Serena eyed me wryly. "Best go with him. My *daed's* as stubborn as they come."

This discarded *docher* must have dug deep into Timothy's heart, because he squeezed my hand and said he might need his little evangelist with him, emphasizing 'angel.' Never knew that word was tucked away in that word. *Ach*, Timothy needed my help. I was his helpmate and my soul felt so satisfied.

~*~

That night we visited Asa. Like we planned, Ivy would be away, with the help of Lena, so she would not hear our confrontation about the photograph. Timothy wrapped on the side door even though we could see Asa reading by oil light at the kitchen table. He was slumped and looked worn out. Maybe we should have done this in the morning, I wondered.

Asa opened the door, surprised to see us. "Thought it was Bishop Dan."

"Are you expecting him?" Timothy asked.

"He stops over from time to time."

"We need to talk to you about something serious," Timothy stated. This was not a suggestion. Asa stepped aside, and we took seats around the soft glow of the lamp.

"Ivy's gone over to Lena's or I'd have her get *yinz* something. Coffee?"

"*Nee*," we said in unison.

Timothy slid the photograph into the bright ring of light. "Found this in our barn."

Asa gasped. "I've been looking for it." His unsteady hand caressed the picture. "She's my sister," he was too quick to say.

"Your sister? So, she's Old Order Mennonite?" I asked, knowing he was lying. No one looked so fondly at a sister.

"*Jah*, I suppose," he said flatly.

"You suppose?" I prodded.

"Sister in the Lord," he confessed. "This is my first wife. I almost forgot what she looked like and someone from back home found it and sent it out. I'm afraid I'll forget the one who brought out goodness in me. Since she's been gone..."

Timothy and I sat silent for a spell. Was he admitting he lacked goodness now? I waited for Timothy to take the lead, but there was no need. Apparently, Asa wanted to talk.

"Rachel and I were what the English call 'soulmates.' We understood each other. We loved each other. So, when I lose hope, I'll look at this picture and thank God I had one *gut* marriage."

This was starting to answer my questions about his *dochders*. He had one *gut* marriage, but not to Ivy, and he took it out on her and the girls. But they could learn to love each other. "Does Ivy know about this picture?"

94

"*Jah*, I told her it's my sister." He scratched the back of his neck. "No one else knows. I married Ivy out of need."

"You had young *kinner*?" Timothy asked, his voice laced with grace.

"*Nee*, she did. Will you vow not to tell a soul our secret?"

"We don't vow to anything," Timothy said, "but we'd like to help you."

He twisted up his lips. "Ivy had Rose out of wedlock. Serena's mine. My bishop wanted to hide Ivy's disgrace, so we wed before she showed. But folks got real suspicious when Ivy opened her big mouth," he growled. "Gave up living in Montana for that woman and she's not one bit grateful. I put a roof over her head, took in the most stubborn child God ever created and now she's rubbed off on Serena." He clenched his fists. "Sometimes, I just want to take off and leave. Go back to Montana."

Even I was speechless. We'd misjudged Asa. Such a hurting man!

"Confession is *gut* for the soul and now we can help bear this burden. Need to get to know *yinz* better, too."

Timothy encouraged. "How about we get together and play board games. Lots of talking gets done over a *gut* game of Scrabble."

Asa swooshed at the air. "Ivy may change. She's young. But you can't teach old dogs new tricks."

"Come again?" Timothy said.

"I'm pushing sixty, while Ivy's only forty."

"You're sixty?" I exclaimed. "*Ach*, you don't look it, but Ivy does. I thought *yinz* were the same age." I cupped my mouth to suppress more babbling.

"I agree," Timothy said, coming to my rescue. "Asa, you're in *gut* shape for sixty."

"I'm pushing sixty, not there yet."

My throat constricted as I bit back tears. Ivy looked much older. The years hadn't been kind. Asa had admitted he lacked goodness. All his rants about putting a roof over Ivy's head, something you'd do for a barn animal, sank me low. "Asa, I think Ivy has a crushed spirit. Maybe she's still ashamed about having a *kinner* out of wedlock, but Jesus said a bruised reed he would not break and a smoldering wick he won't snuff out. God can give you love for Ivy."

Another dismissive swoosh. "I tried at first, but she compared me with her old boyfriend, of all things. I liked her enough to marry her, but seemed like all I did was wrong. I knew I was being compared and well, it snuffed me out. She snuffs me out daily." His brows furrowed, and his eyes darted from me and then to Timothy. "Will you tell Bishop Dan about this picture?"

"Will you try to breathe some life into your marriage and your *dochders*?" I pressed, a bit too hard.

Timothy rubbed my back. "You confessed a lot tonight. Now, the biggest sin is not having this photograph, but you living in the past. You've got to learn to love your wife and *dochders*. Serena should be living here, not with us. How's that for starters? Put on kindness and be gentle."

"Ivy and I just grit and bear. Serena thinks Rose is her full sister, and lately, Ivy's been talking about needing to confess. That Lena King sure does have a way of swaying Ivy."

I wanted to defend Lena immediately, but kept my peace. God was doing something here. Ivy was being transparent around Lena and Lena knew the truth set her free. Ivy would be free if she didn't keep such secrets. This secret was a yoke too heavy to bear.

Timothy drummed his fingers on the table. "If you have no intention of changing, I need to tell Bishop Dan. Maybe he can help."

"He's tried. Even he doesn't know how to help."

"They have Christian counseling at the Mennonite Center," I said. "Maybe a professional can help. Maybe you need to work on communication skills?"

Asa slapped the table. "Mennonites! How do you know? Too cozy with them."

"Hold on now," Timothy warned. "Don't talk to Ruth like that. We all know we get help from Mennonites. We use Mennonite midwives."

Asa shot up and grabbed a pitcher of iced tea from the icebox. "Let me think about it, but I doubt it. Playing cards or a game with *yinz* could lighten up this…burial ground."

Burial ground? Such harsh words. How does he speak to Ivy? *Lord, have mercy on this family!*

~*~

The next day while Lena came over for morning coffee and a quick prayer, I needed two cups of strong black coffee, but stuck to one while being pregnant. I tossed half the night, and when I wasn't, Timothy was.

"What is it?" Lena asked. "You look shaken. *Boppli* okay?"

"*Jah*, they are."

Lena laughed. "You may not be having twins! Now, tell me."

It was hopeless. Lena saw right through me. "I'm worried about Ivy and Asa. Asa told us some disturbing stories last night, I can't share. Gave my word. But, how does Ivy live with that man?"

Lena's eyes glazed. "You learn to survive, like I did with Samson. Ivy's opening up, too. Telling me secrets about her past."

"About…Rose?"

"*Jah*. She carries so much guilt; Asa has always treated her like an immoral woman."

"*Jah*. But Asa said he tried to love her, but she compared him to Rose's *daed*."

Lena's eyes grew round. "You're defending Asa?"

"Well, seems like he had good intentions. Do you know he's nearly sixty and Ivy's only forty?"

Pity and empathy were etched into Lena's brow. "*Nee*, I didn't know, but I understand how you can age with constant browbeating."

"He says she's not too kind to him." One of the *boppli* kicked, jolting me. "We best not argue over this. *Bopplin's* kicking for me to calm down."

"We're not arguing, Ruth. I just don't think you understand the state of mind Ivy is in. She's worse than I was when under Samson's iron fist. *Ach*, being married to Jacob is bliss. It's what a marriage should be. When I see Ivy, I see me, I suppose. But she's lacking something mighty important. The will to live."

"She said that?"

"*Nee*, but I can tell. This estrangement from her *dochders* caused by Asa has made her so low. She said the other day she can't wait to go home to glory. Is that normal?"

"People say that all the time, but in Ivy's case, I suppose it shows how hopeless she is. Maybe Asa's idea is *gut*. Timothy and I will go over and visit more, sowing seeds of hope. Maybe something will grow?"

Lena grabbed my hands and we sat in silent prayer. *Why did I care so much about other people's problems?* I asked

God. Was I meddlesome or did he put compassion into my makeup? I tried to quiet my mind by repeating my Breath Prayers. *Lord, have mercy. Your will be done. Come Lord Jesus. Heal our land. Heal Asa and Ivy's marriage.* I felt myself calm down and listened to the robin sing its morning song. God looked after birds and he surely could see what was going on over at the Coblenz house.

Lena said "Amen" and I rose to start my day, but Lena remained on the bench. "Ruth, any mail from Falcon Hill?"

"*Nee.* No letter from Becky yet?"

Lena stood and smoothed out wrinkles from her apron. "*Nee.* And I think I've written my last. I need to step back and wait for God to fight for me."

"Fight for you? Lena, you sound like an Evangelical."

Lena smiled. "Something I saw in Exodus. Moses told the Israelites, 'The Lord will fight for you. You only need to remain silent.' And then the Red Sea parted. That's a mighty miracle and that's what it's going to take for Becky to stop being so stubborn."

Such pain in Lena's voice. I took her hands. "I've been writing to Becky, too. It wasn't my place, but I thought I could help."

Lena surprised me by kissing my hands. "You are my sister. The best one ever."

We embraced, and I thought back to how much I wanted to have Lena and Jacob live next door. It all seemed like we'd live in total peace. But being neighbors with the Coblenz family was draining us both. The scripture she'd said about the Lord fighting the battle and us remaining silent seemed mighty appealing. But, could I ever remain silent?

Chapter 8

Timothy was flustered when he came in for the noon meal because I heard him kick off his boots in the utility room and then something fell and then more noise. My husband was in a rush about something. And he only rushed when upset. "Something wrong?" I yelled from the kitchen.

He appeared, glaring like never before. I stopped what I was doing. "What has Asa done now?"

He yanked his beard and paced, trying to gain composure. "It's you, Ruth."

"Me? What are you talking about?"

"Talking. How appropriate. Talking. Want to confess anything?"

I neared him to feel his forehead. "No temperature. What is wrong with you?"

"Talking, Ruth. What do people talk on?"

"Talk on? Talk on the weather and…the Bible? Did I preach too much again? Bishop Dan say something about me being too pushy at knitting circle?"

He huffed. "*Nee*. Sit down."

I wanted to say I wasn't one of his dogs, but this was so out of character for Timothy that I obeyed.

He pulled something out of his pocket and slammed it on the table. "This rang when Asa came over to thank us for visiting. Asa knew how it worked and answered it when the name 'Rose' came up. Before Asa could say anything, Rose began crying. Lost her job and wants to move back to Punxsy."

I lowered my head and let it rest on my palms. "Sorry, Timothy. I forgot to tell you about it. Serena had it in her room and I agreed to her keeping it in the barn."

"Ruth Miller, do you realize how much trouble we could be in?"

I didn't care about confessing to letting Serena have a cellphone in the barn. She had good reasons. Timothy was afraid I'd never stop being so suspicious. Always on the fence with modern ways or Ex-Amish. "I'm sorry I disappointed you. I know I'm a challenge."

He softened enough to get iced tea from the icebox and sit across from me. "You never disappoint me, Ruth. I'm sorry. Asa went off, threatening to tell Bishop Dan and it brings back memories of Falcon Hill."

"I'll confess to letting Serena keep the phone…in the barn…like Amish businesses are allowed."

Timothy reached for my hand. "Rose sounded so scared. She's out there on her own, *jah*? No job; no one to fall back on."

"No family. It's why I feel so much for those two girls."

He laced his fingers through mine. "You're heavy on the nest. You talk about those two girls as if they were your *kinner*."

"You're right. I do have motherly feelings for them. Who wouldn't?"

Just then the cellphone rang, and I picked it up and saw the name *Rose*. I just couldn't answer it. "I'm so afraid I'm going to spill the beans about her real birth *daed*. It's still such a shock."

"She'll need a place to stay if she lost her job, but I agree. Not here. She could overhear."

"Aunt Naomi said she's looking for some help at The Secret Garden B&B. Maybe Rose could help in exchange for rent?"

~*~

The next few days, I expected Bishop Dan to appear, giving me a warning, but all was quiet for a spell. I knit two *boppli* hats in one day, just in case. Today I was in my garden shed, dropping tomato and pepper seeds into the potting soil, and I pondered seeds. It was a miracle each time the little green sprout sprang up, a sign of resurrection. Seeds were dead, but when swelled with water, they broke open, letting loose the embryo of life. I thought of Lena and how she had been dried up like a dead seed being married to Samson. But with Jacob, she was growing, standing tall like corn stalks.

But what about Ivy? Could Lena really help her? I thought about The Parable of the Sower and the Seeds. Some seeds fell among thorns and when they tried to grow, the thorns ate them up. Asa was choking Ivy. How I dreaded going over to play Scrabble tonight. *Ach, Lord, help me see Asa through Your eyes. I admit, he's as prickly as a thorn, but I can't let him get to me. I know I should pray for him, and I will, but please, protect me from that man eating me up.*

In my little shed, the large windows were lined with shelves to house plants. I could see the trees budding already, a sign of an early spring, even though late March. Folks back in Falcon Hill were buried in snow, for sure. I never had doubts that we made the move to Pennsylvania for more than a longer growing season.

I spied a young Amish man coming down the road in an open buggy, slowing down to a stop. In no time, Serena had run out of the house and hopped into the buggy. *Ach*, courting was only after Singings. What was the girl thinking? And who was the young man? If she wanted to live under our roof, there'd be rules to follow.

Just then I saw Ivy come running out of her house, her hand over her mouth, and she looked mighty defeated. I dusted soil from my gardening apron and rushed outside to see what was wrong. "Ivy, what is it?"

"Serena's seeing Levi?" she gasped, fear pinching her brow.

"Is that who just picked her up?"

"*Jah.* And he's a bad influence. Made Rose leave the Amish."

A shadow darkened the sky and it started to drizzle. "Do you want to come back to my garden shed and talk about it?" Ivy nodded, and we hurried in before we got poured on. "April showers brings May flowers, *jah*?"

"It's not April until next week," Ivy said flatly. "*Ach*, Ruth, wish I could live in this little spot and hide from the world. Asked Asa to build me a garden shed ten years ago or more. Never did. Wants me trapped in my kitchen. No wonder the girls left."

Was I hearing right? She was being transparent, not wearing a mask? "So, you and Asa have your differences?"

"Do we ever. And now that it's just the two of us at home, it's so lonely. Lena coming over helps. Both of *yinz* do. I shouldn't complain. The old neighbors weren't too friendly."

We settled into chairs and listened to the rain hit the metal roof. "Life never turns out like we plan it. But God works everything together for the *gut*," I said. "Romans 8:28. I depend on that verse for my sanity sometimes."

"Are you having troubles with Timothy?"

"*Ach, nee*. We're still newlyweds in a way. Married only over two years. Haven't raised *kinner* yet. What I mean is sometimes I feel like a misfit person. Most women feel so content to just cook, clean and be a homemaker. I love to be creative, spinning wool or knitting or sewing. And I love animals a bit too much. Trying to convince Timothy to let me have an indoor cat, but he says they belong outside."

Ivy started to bite her nails. "No one knows what a misfit I am. Never fit into this settlement."

I suspected Asa kept her from getting out much, lest she slip and tell someone Rose was not his *dochder*. "Come to knitting circle tomorrow. You need to be friendly to make friends."

"Asa won't let me."

"You ask permission?" I blurted. "Ivy, are you serious?"

"I went to plenty years ago but stopped going. Asa came out one day and said he didn't want the girls and me to go to any frolics. Plenty to do at home."

I sighed. "No wonder the girls are so angry. You three lived like caged birds."

Ivy burst into tears. "I ruined my girls."

I clasped her hand. "They're fine girls. You raised them *gut*. Just because Rose isn't Amish doesn't mean you failed."

"Asa's too hard on her," she blubbered. "And it's all my fault."

I embraced her, letting her cry on my shoulder. How this reminded me of Lena when she revealed being in a most unhappy marriage. *Lord, help Asa see what a treasure he has in Ivy.*

~*~

Serena strayed in for supper. She apologized for getting held up visiting Old Anna May Yoder, a widow folks made sure had plenty of company. We all sat, and Timothy led in a silent prayer, clearing his throat when done. I liked to air things out, not let things fester….and I was festering.

"Your *Mamm* said Levi took you to Anna May Yoder's."

Choking, Serena slowly sipped down iced tea. "She saw us?"

"I saw *yinz*, too. You were cooped up growing up, but we have rules, too. No courting unless after a Singing." I looked to Timothy for support, but he was hunched over his meal, ravished.

"I'm not courting Levi," Serena insisted. "He just gave me a ride."

"You can walk to Old Anna May's from here. Less than a mile. Now, Serena, if you're going to live here, we need honesty. Tell me the truth."

"Promise you won't tell anyone."

"*Nee*, we can't do that," Timothy said. "Might not be able to keep quiet. If you've done nothing wrong, why not just say it?"

Serena poked at her pot roast. "He drove me over to see Rose."

"Rose?" Timothy and I asked in unison.

"*Jah*. Rose lost her job but got one right quick at New Life Church on Main Street. Levi wanted to see her, too."

I was leaving it up to Serena to tell us about Rose's call and was relieved she spoke up. "Where's she staying?"

"She's staying over at the Secret Garden B&B. She's doing extra chores in exchange for rent. Naomi and Micah are so kind."

"They helped us see we needed to settle here," Timothy said.

"*Jah*, they did," I said. "Maybe they can convince Rose she should return to her Amish roots."

"She's evangelical," Serena said. "She told Levi all kinds of stuff about knowing Jesus like a friend. His ears pricked right up."

Timothy laughed. "He liked your sister before and her pretty voice pricked his ears up. Lots of Amish call Jesus 'friend.'"

"Not like how Rose talks. And she invited him to a church service. He's not baptized yet, and he agreed on it."

Why did I feel nervous, like I was harboring a new rebellion? "Serena, I don't want to hear anything about Levi and this church. You know we lived over at The Secret Garden B&B when fifteen-some Amish left to be Mennonite. We were really looked at with suspicion as if we encouraged it. And poor Naomi and Micah can only rent to Amish and trusted English friends now."

Timothy tapped his butter knife on the table. "Serena, if you encourage your sister to invite Amish to this evangelical church, you can't live here, plain and simple. I hear the fear in Ruth's voice and she's pregnant. Don't want her nerves on edge."

Serena's eyes watered up and she mashed her lips together. Her chin quivered as she got up from the table. "I'll go pack my things."

Timothy caught her by the shoulder. "Honey, I'm so tired from fixing all those fences. Now, don't leave us on bad terms. We like having you here and care about you."

Serena sat again, but her crossed arms and rigid frame said she'd rather skedaddle over to the B&B.

"Would you like to go back home? Your *mamm* misses you."

She gasped. "She does? *Ach*, sometimes I do, but my *daed* is so mean. And Rose can't visit. So strange it's embarrassing to be a part of my family." She readjusted her prayer *kapp*, making it way too lopsided to the left.

"How about you play a board game with us tonight? See how you feel. We're seeing some change in your *daed*."

Serena stared aimlessly ahead. "*Nee*, I need to go. Maybe I can stay with Old Anna May. She needs help getting around and has a spare room. Truth is, I told Rose I was going to New Life Church with Levi."

I near fell off the chair. *Poor Ivy! She's mighty low. This will do her in!* I heard Timothy tell Serena she could leave in the morning, no rush to leave tonight.

~*~

Ivy didn't want to play a game, feeling tired, so we awkwardly sat outside on the porch, listening to the peeper frogs who sang out too loud at times. We sipped meadow tea and Ivy passed around store bought cookies. I wanted to mention that the stars were so vivid, a cloudless night, and perhaps Timothy could bring over his telescope. The only sound was the deafening squeaking of the glider Ivy and Asa reluctantly shared. I slid next to Timothy. "There's a chill in the air."

"Do you want hot tea?" Ivy asked.

"*Nee*, this is fine," I said, raising my glass.

Timothy shifted, his uneasiness evident. "I have a request."

"I'll put the kettle on," Ivy said, gingerly rising like an elderly woman.

"*Nee*, not hot tea, but a different request." He pulled a little Bible out of his pocket, opened it and read:

I therefore, the prisoner of the Lord, beg you to walk worthily of the calling with which you were called, with all lowliness and humility, with patience, bearing with one another in love; being eager to keep the unity of the Spirit in the bond of peace.

"That's Ephesians 4:1-2. Now, live a life worthy of being called a Christian. Be patient, love each other, create a home filled with peace!"

I sat back stunned at Timothy's boldness. A few times he hit his knee to emphasize a point.

"You come over to my house to insult me?" Asa accused.

"I came over here mad, is what. I have your *dochder*, Serena, who's as sweet as the day is long, wanting to live with you if there wasn't a war going on." He shot up and paced. "But most likely she'll go over and live with Old Anna May Yoder."

"Why's she leaving your place?" Ivy peeped.

"Because she doesn't want to put us in a difficult position," Timothy said evenly. "We wouldn't want to be harboring a rebellion."

Asa slammed his fist against the glider. "Told you she was rebellious. Having a cellphone."

"Not that!" I near screamed. "She wants to go to an *Englisher* church with…. Rose. That's where she went with Levi."

"I don't understand. Rose lives in Pittsburgh."

"She got a job at New Life Church in town. And if I were you, I'd go after her and make peace. It might just make Serena want to come live back home."

"New Life Church?" Ivy gasped. "I hear they dance in the aisles."

"Forget all that." Timothy clapped his hands as if to wake them up. "See the big picture." He faced Asa. "Love Rose like your own. Put on humility and make peace, like the Bible says. She's not baptized."

Ivy put her head in her hands and groaned.

"I'm sorry, Ivy, I don't mean to be so unkind, but Serena's really hurting," Timothy said.

"Asa, you told them Rose isn't yours?" She hunkered down in shame. "And you said I'd be the one blabbing it."

"Well, Ivy," I said, "how does Lena know?"

Asa's eyes grew wide, the light of the oil lamp flickering in them. "You told Lena?"

"Just Lena, but she told *yinz?*" Ivy said evenly, pointing to us.

"What difference does it make?" Timothy said, trying to bring everyone back on topic. "So, your new neighbors know, and we don't judge. Why, Asa, do you judge? Why, Ivy, don't you forgive yourself?"

They grew quiet and Timothy sat down next to me. I was glad a nightingale began to sing, something of a diversion. The glider began to squeak again.

"You don't judge?" Asa asked.

"He who is without sin, cast the first stone," Timothy said.

Ivy held her heart as tears streamed down her face. Asa did nothing to comfort her but set his jaw. "Tell Serena to come home where she belongs," Asa said. "I can see Ivy needs her here."

Asa was an odd creature, so hard to read. Did he want Serena to come back as a loving gesture to Ivy, or would she be a buffer between them? Timothy must have picked up my thoughts because he asked this very question. Asa said he'd try to make the home as peaceful as possible for Serena's sake. But his voice was low and strained, and something told me to tell Serena to go live with Old Anna May Yoder. *Ach, I'll tell her everything and she can decide. She's not my kinner.*

Chapter 9

As April drizzled across the rolling hills of Pennsylvania, the rain bringing much needed water to trees that were now starting to blossom, I hoped the same for Serena. I hoped she blossomed over at her parent's house. Bloom where you're planted, my *grossmammi* always said. *Lord, I pray Serena can bloom in her home.*

When I spied Aunt Naomi's black buggy come up the driveway, I picked up my canvas bag. But, I had to take a double-look. It wasn't a buggy but a black shiny van. I pulled back the white curtain to see New Life Church painted on the van. *Ach, nee!* Folks will think I'm going to that church! I opened the door and startled Rose, who was about to knock.

"Are you ready to go shopping?"

"I thought Naomi would bring her buggy."

"It's windy and we'll get drenched. Naomi thinks she's coming down with a spring cold."

I wanted to say we have rolldown flaps to keep the rain off in our buggies, but Rose knew this. Aunt Naomi came to the door, urging me to get under her umbrella and into the van. Before I knew it, we were headed throughout Amish country in an Evangelical church van.

"Too bad my parents won't let Serena be in the van," Rose said. "It's all I have to drive until my car gets fixed."

So, Asa knew about our shopping trip…and getting there in this van. "How does Serena look?"

Rose's cheeks puffed up with air and sighed it out audibly. "*Mamm* wasn't home, which is odd. I think she went over to Lena's for something. *Daed* said Serena had too many chores to do to come to the door."

I felt my forehead tense up and I tried to relax, not wanting a headache. "Was he mean to you?"

"Is he anything but? Never knew such a mean man. And he has the audacity to cut down Levi."

Aunt Naomi looked back at me, eyebrows up. "Timothy and Jacob are working on him. Mighty *gut* examples of men who love their wives." She let her eyes land on Rose. "Are you courting Levi Hostetler?"

Rose shrugged. "We're friends. I know he's trying to get me to come back to the People, so I invited him to my church. No offense to the Amish, but I don't plan on being plain."

"And you want Levi to be evangelical?" I asked.

"I don't know what I want. So much change lately. Losing my job and now making less than half of what I'm used to, all I can think of is how to be frugal and simplify. Try to find culture out here in the boonies."

"What do you mean by culture?" Aunt Naomi asked.

"Oh, I miss the theater, concerts, fine dining. Even ballroom dancing. I know it sounds carnal to *yinz*, but I could never give it up." Rose turned the windshield wipers on full speed as the rain poured onto the van. "Glad we're not in a buggy."

"Me, too," Aunt Naomi said. "But can you slow down? There's little streams forming on the road."

Rose bit her lower lip. "Looks like we may have some flash flooding."

"*Ach*, I hope not," I exclaimed. "I planted snow peas and other early crops. The seeds could wash away."

Lightning flashed and banged, and I was indeed glad to be in this car. We skid going around a curve, but regained traction. A coal truck passed by and I thanked the Lord we'd not crossed over into the other lane. I was relieved when we got into town and Rose found a parking spot close to The Country Store. I looked across the street to see the red brick Mennonite church, where Stephen and Sarah, along with other ex-Amish, attended. Did my eyes deceive me? I wiped the fogged-up windows so I could see clearly. There was a sign in the church window reading, *FREE MEDICAL CARE IF IN NEED.* Free? Medical care in a church?

I held my middle, just knowing I was carrying twins. "I'd like to go over to the Mennonite church. There's a sign saying free medical care. Naomi, maybe Stephen could check you to see if you have a spring cold. He must be in there if that sign's up."

Aunt Naomi spun around, glaring at me in disbelief. "After all we've been through? Ruth, we must be careful. I never want to be accused of starting a rift between the People again."

Rose looked at me with pity. "You have questions about your baby, don't you? And you want a real medical professional to see you?"

"*Jah*," I found myself saying. "I really do. I think I'm carrying twins. Maybe Stephen can put that heartbeat thing to my stomach and hear two heartbeats."

"That would be interesting," Aunt Naomi confessed.

~*~

I near sprang out of the van when Rose pulled into my house. "Timothy!" I yelled, wondering if he was outside. I waved good-bye to Rose and Aunt Naomi and scurried towards the barn. "Timothy!" Only the squealing of my baby piglets, bleating of sheep and cow's mooing. "Timothy!"

Nowhere to be found, until I heard my name being yelled from Asa's buggy repair shop. Call it hormones, pure adrenaline, or plain old excitement, but I darted to him, jogging while holding my watermelon belly. Well, cantaloupe, really. I waved my hand overhead, praising God. And I didn't care one hoot if Asa heard.

"What is it? Get a *gut* sale on yarn?" Timothy quipped.

I laughed. "*Nee*, and I spin my own. Now, Timothy, you need to sit down."

"Calm down, Ruth. You're scaring me." He sat on a nearby tree stump. "Okay, I'm sitting."

I clapped my hands and stomped my feet. "I was right! God told me I was having twins!"

Timothy's mouth gaped. "What?"

"I got a fetal Doppler done at the Mennonite Church's new health clinic. No charge. And Stephen heard two heartbeats! Can't tell if we have boys or girls, but an ultrasound can tell." I arched my neck and admired the blue sky. "God is so *gut*! We got a late start, so he's giving us twins!"

Timothy's eyes narrowed into slits, while Asa stomped out of his shop. Asa looked mighty irritated. Maybe a hard buggy to fix?

"Can someone say congratulations?" I asked.

"I'm in shock, Ruth," Timothy said. "Don't know what to make of it. Don't know if I believe those medical gadgets work right."

"I know what to make of it," Asa boomed. "*Yinz* are too cozy with modern ways and Ex-Amish. Stephen Byler led that rebellion and you're still friendly, *jah*? Well, you can tell a lot about someone by the friends they keep, the Bible says."

Timothy shot up. "Asa, that's taken out of context. We're not best friends with Stephen and Sarah."

Asa started to raise one finger at a time, listing all our transgressions. "Glory Barn, cellphone in the house, riding in that wild church's van, and now, being a prophet of God."

"Prophet of God?" I humphed. "What on earth!"

"You said God spoke to you. Told you, personally, that you were having twins. Don't prophets hear from God…in the Old Testament? Ruth, I can't ignore your behavior anymore, but will be having a talking to with Bishop Dan."

I clenched my fists. "I can list off a few of your obvious transgressions, like being too harsh with your wife. Why pray? God's not going to hear you the way you treat your wife and *dochders*."

"Ruth," Timothy gasped.

"It's the truth. I can't stand a hypocrite. You're an actor, Asa. That's what a hypocrite means. How come Serena couldn't go with us shopping today? Because you rule with an iron fist, and let me see… I think I can tell the future, like a prophet! She's going to move out again!"

"Your face is too red, Ruth." Timothy turned me around, leading me over to our place. "I've never seen you in such a state. Please, calm down."

I leaned into Timothy and cried, letting all my anger and vexation out. "Asa will…drive…me…nuts!"

We sat on our porch glider and Timothy let it sway us back and forth and I felt like a *kinner*, being rocked so I'd calm down.

"Everything you said was true, honey. It's time Asa's held accountable for his poor character. Just when you think he's making progress."

"He's a wolf in sheep's clothing," I spouted. "And when I calm down, we're going over to Bishop Dan's and tell him all we know. Rose and Serena have given me an earful."

"*Shh*," Timothy cooed. "I don't know if I'll have time to see Bishop Dan. Seems like I need to make this farm produce more, since we'll be a family of four."

His voice broke with emotion. He believed me. I knew Timothy believed in Stephen and the fetal Doppler but was most likely in shock. I was so happy to give this man a family. I secretly hoped they were boys that looked just like him.

~*~

We decided to wait a few days before visiting Bishop Dan, but Asa had gone the day of our big fight and now, here we were, Bishop Dan sitting across our table, twiddling his thumbs. "So, Ruth, is all this true? I do know you got a warning in Falcon Hill for being too Evangelical."

I glanced up to see the dismay on Timothy's face. We had to move because of my behavior before. Will we have to again? Turn Mennonite? "Bishop Dan, some of what Asa says is exaggerated. I never claimed God told me I was having twins, like a prophet. It was my motherly intuition. I did go to the Glory Barn revival, desperate to be healed. And I believe I was. I believe God opened my womb."

Timothy started to massage his temples.

"Serena had a cellphone so Rose could contact her, but I believed cellphones were allowed for business, if kept in the barn. Was I wrong to let her keep it in the barn?"

Bishop Dan shook his head. "Only for businesses to make money to provide for a family. Not for communicating. We don't want phone calls to replace visiting."

"But Serena can't visit Rose," I protested. "And the Coblenz girls are hurting so much. They need each other."

Timothy put his hand on mine, squeezing it. This was his signal that I'd best be quiet. "More coffee?" I asked. "Want some cookies?"

Bishop Dan's face dropped. "*Danki* but *nee*. I've been fasting over many issues. Since the rebellion, I've talked to many in the *Gmay*. What the People need is more Bible learning." He threw up his hands. "Maybe I need to confess that I've been talking to Stephen and Sarah Byler, too, trying to get them to see our ways, so they'd come back. But..."

"But?"

"I find myself tempted to try to adapt some of their ways into our *Gmay* while still being Old Order Amish. Our People's history is rich with faith in Jesus. Many lost their lives. But I see many just going through vain traditions. *Jah*, we need more Bible learning."

Timothy cleared his throat, apparently nervous. "Do you want to turn Beachy Amish? New Order?"

Bishop Dan shook his head vehemently. "*Nee*, not at all. But from what *yinz* are saying is Asa has a Christian character problem, let's just say it for what it is. *Sin*. And he comes over here telling me Ruth was a passenger in New Life Church's van, as if we're all ruled by...rules.

That's easy. The Pharisees did that." He scratched the back of his neck as his face deepened into a dark crimson. "Asa's been a handful. I'm not blind. I see how Stephen treats Sarah, and it's God-honoring." He pounded the table. "That's what I'm getting at. We need to be more God-honoring."

Just then, Serena came in the side door, tears running down her cheeks. "Can I live here again?"

Bishop Dan, filled with compassion, got up and offered Serena his clean handkerchief. "Now, now. It's going to be okay. I'll be giving your *daed* a talking to. He needs to honor God more in his daily life. Treat his *dochders* better."

"He's not Rose's *daed*!" Serena turned, facing us. "I overheard *yinz* talk and I asked my *mamm*. She told me the truth." She eyed Bishop Dan. "How could you treat my *mamm* with such *unforgiveness*? She's not a bad woman. Why did you say no one was to talk to Rose?"

Bishop Dan became trance-like. "Asa's not Rose's *daed*?" He put his head between his knees, starting to sway. Timothy led him to a chair and the bishop collapsed into it.

Serena came to my side, fear that she'd pushed the bishop too far. "Everything I said is true," she whispered in my ear.

"I never told folks not to talk to Rose," the bishop said in monotone. "Asa planted some wicked seeds into the minds of the People about that poor girl. No wonder she's turned to the world for comfort." He put his head in his hands. "I need to make things right. I've been a blind bishop."

I wanted to say Asa pulled the wool over his eyes, but was trying to keep calm, for my *bopplin's* sake. I thought of how my white sheets and towels got a natural bleaching by being hung out in the sun to dry. This blot that Asa had put on his family needed to be aired out, the stains removed. *Lord, help Bishop Dan gain strength to do what's right.*

Chapter 10

A week went by and all the People had one thing on their mind. Where did Bishop Dan and his wife go? No word left to church leadership, and it was fast approaching Easter. Some folks needed to be reconciled and the bishop would help in the process. Timothy and I knew he left the day after our talk about Asa, and the bishop did look ill. Did he take a time of rest?

Lena and I decided to shake off our concerns with pie. We baked so many we had enough to sell in front of The Country Store. Serena and Ivy knew how to make fudge, and they asked if they could join our bake sale. Rose was often seen driving the church van to our place to drop off more baking supplies.

I noticed a change in Ivy since she told Rose the details of her birth. Rose seemed to walk with her head a bit higher, happy Asa wasn't her real father. *Such a man,* she often said. When Serena parroted Rose, Ivy put them in their places, but did not defend him like she used to. She asked that we pray for him and she was determined to show him the love of God.

Word quickly got out among the People concerning Rose and many stopped by New Life Church to embrace her, asking for forgiveness for judging her wrongly. Many believed she was so rebellious, like Asa had portrayed her. Some dared to stop over and beg Ivy to attend quilting bees. *Ach*, Ivy's guilt was lifting, praise be. The only one who was being severely judged, near shunned by the People, was Asa. Ivy said the elders came and gave him a talking to. She heard them say, "Asa, your deceit and how you've treated your women-folk is more sinful than Ivy's long past transgression."

Timothy steered clear of Asa until he could get over how poorly he treated Serena when she went home for a short stay. He didn't want to speak out of anger, so he said nothing. Jacob King, kind as ever, did go over and offered to be Asa's friend. I wanted to go over, too. I wanted to be that angel Timothy talked about. Eva Angel...

Today, I hoped our bake sale at The Country Store would take my mind off Bishop Dan. Where on earth did he disappear to? Did the People need to file a missing person's report?

~*~

Lena, Rose, and I manned the bake sale booth, Ivy and Serena needing some mother-daughter time. By lunchtime, the table was half empty, but we had plenty to restock. But those clouds, those dark wispy clouds, started to float in, and once again, I couldn't get over how unpredictable the weather was in Western Pennsylvania. The temperature dropped suddenly, and the wind kicked up. I waved to Stephen when he came to close the front door of the Mennonite church and take down the sign for free counseling. I waved for him to come over, which he did.

"Take your pick. No charge," I said. "We have banana cream pie."

He grinned. "You know I have a weakness for that. Did Aunt Naomi make it?"

"*Nee*, Lena did."

The wind blew up our tablecloth, flipping the cupcake tray. Stephen tried to hold down the table, but said we best be taking the baked goods to his church. He offered to put an "Amish Bake Sale" sign up. It sounded good to us as the drizzle threatened to destroy our goods. Ivy and Serena ran back to the table and we all tore down everything and had the baked goods over at the Mennonite Church in no time. And then the sky broke open like a waterfall.

"*Danki*, Stephen," we all said, trying not to make too much noise. Even though the free counseling sign was down, there were people still at tables being counseled. I saw that a few were Amish. Or were they Old Order Mennonite? Surely, they were Old Order Mennonite, still holding to their horse and buggy ways. But the back of one head I seemed to recognize. Bishop Dan?

As our table was set up again inside the simple, plain church, very similar to the interior of Amish homes, I pulled Stephen aside and asked to have a counseling session. Lena overheard and eyed me with a glare, but I just nodded, letting her know everything was okay. She understood. We could read each other like real sisters.

Stephen led me to one of the tables, and I caught a glimpse of Bishop Dan. What on earth?

"How can I help you, Ruth? You look troubled."

I was so dumbfounded, I only sputtered out, "Bishop Dan. He's here?"

Stephen slowly closed his eyes. "Yes. He's been staying here."

"I, ah, I don't understand. Why would he do that? Everyone's looking for him or wondering if he needed a long vacation. We thought he went to Lancaster to visit kin, but he never left word to the elders." I wrung my hands. "Asa Coblenz brought him to the end of his rope, *jah*? He came here, hiding, to get some rest?"

Stephen crossed his arms. "When at the end of your rope, sometimes you see more clearly." He licked his lips, appearing very nervous. "Ruth, he said you spoke truth to him, and he woke up."

"I what? I didn't wake anyone up."

"He saw real Christian character in you and Timothy when he came to give you a warning. He said you thought character was above the *Ordnung*, which is correct."

"The Bible comes first, but we need order. Rules..."

"Dan feels like he missed the big picture." He opened his thick Bible, highlighted in lots of yellow and words written in the margins. "Listen to this:

"He has told you, O man, what is good; And what does the Lord require of you except to be just, and to love and to diligently

practice kindness, compassion, and to walk humbly with your God, setting aside any overblown sense of importance or self-righteousness?

"That's the Amplified Version, but you may simply know it as, *What doth the Lord require of thee but to do justly and to love mercy, and to walk humbly with thy God?"*

I nodded, knowing that scripture, pondering it often. "So, Dan is here on a retreat, learning the Bible? Getting himself built-up to go through the Easter season?"

Stephen took my hands, as if to brace me for something. "He believes what the Mennonites believe. He's had the gift of evangelism and he recognized it when he met you."

"*Nee*, this can't be true!" I withdrew my hands. "I never taught him the Bible."

"He saw a rare joy in you when talking about Jesus."

"But I didn't preach from the Bible," I huffed, rather too defensively.

"Not chapter and verse, but you did share basic themes, right? It's in your heart, Ruth, so it comes out. '*Out of the abundance of the heart, the mouth speaks?'* You've hidden God's Word in your heart, and it comes out. I admire that."

I began to tremble and my heart near beat out of my chest. The warning I received in New York flashed before me. "Is Bishop Dan leaving the Amish?" I panicked.

"Ruth, I'm sorry. Looks that way. He'll step down as bishop —"

"You can't step down as a bishop!"

"He can if he's not Amish."

"Not Amish?" Anger erupted within. "Stephen, he was so vulnerable. So beaten down. You talked him out of being Amish?"

"He sought us out. Knocked on our door and Sarah and I just listened. Like I said, he's been feeling like he's supposed to be Evangelical, to preach the Word of God, like we Mennonites do. He'd been talking to Ex-Amish who left not long ago."

So, it wasn't my fault, I reasoned. "Will he tell the People it was the Ex-Amish who persuaded him to leave, not me?"

I was startled when Bishop Dan set a chair next to me and placed an arm on my shoulder. "Ruth, I'll leave you out of this when I tell the elders we're leaving, but I need to thank you. I saw in you what I longed to be, a sower of seeds, an evangelist. And I feel like I'm in my twenties again, so free to be what I've been called to do."

He was glowing, not hunched over like an old man. I couldn't help but feel happy for him. But I feared when others saw this change, there would be another 'rebellion' and many thought I was too cozy with the Mennonites. And Asa knew I went to the Glory Barn! Would the one who drew the lot to be the new bishop have mercy on me?

~*~

The next few days, I tried not to mingle with too many folks, at Timothy's request. He supposed Bishop Dan was so fatigued, maybe he just had a breakdown of sorts. Maybe a crisis of belief, and hoped he'd return to the People. And that's what happened today, on this Lord's Day. He was at *Gmay* and sought Timothy and I out after the service. "I think I found that there's a balance between Amish and Mennonite ways."

"R-really?" Timothy stuttered.

"Met lots of other pastors at the Mennonite Church who fear half their congregations are just going through the motions, so to speak. That it's just a tradition with no heartfelt love for our Lord. One pastor said only twenty-percent of Christians in the USA know their Bibles, the other are considered Biblically illiterate."

My heart dropped into my toes. I couldn't go for a day without reading my Bible. "How can people not read their Bibles?"

"Like I said, just going to church out of habit. One pastor called it a social club, like the YMCA." He smiled hopefully. "Mennonites, too. So, I figured it's like that with the Amish. *Nee*, I won't be giving up on the People, but I'll be encouraging Bible reading in the homes and even groups."

I held on to Timothy as I felt faint. "Am I hearing you right? You're going to encourage Bible studies in the home?"

"Well, let's say I won't be prohibiting free speech, *jah*? If you have a quilting bee and you want to talk about the Bible, feel free." He put his hand on his hips and offered me a grin. "You have the Living Water gushing out of you. You can't help it, *jah*?"

"Timothy, pinch me. I think I'm dreaming."

He pinched my cheek playfully. "No more fears of getting a warning for being Eva Angel."

"Eva Angel?" Bishop Dan questioned.

"Short for Evangelist."

I still couldn't believe all this. "Bishop Dan, the Amish aren't evangelical like the Mennonites. We try to show our faith by our actions."

"Like Stephen said, there's a thirst among the People. It's God who draws us, *jah*? It's not normal to thirst for Bible knowledge, but the Holy Spirit gives us the desire. So, if God's in it, how can we stop it? I say we encourage Bible reading and see how things pan out with the People."

Well, he was our leader, and I wanted to shout for joy. "So, you'll be helping to unite the *Gmay* in preparation for Easter?"

"*Jah*, I'll be doing that all week. Need to see me?"

I sighed audibly. "*Jah*. I have to make peace with Asa."

"Me, too," Timothy said. "That man accused Ruth of sin and tried to cause trouble. Plus, I've come to really like Serena and I see how she's been beaten down by him."

Bishop Dan pulled on his beard. "I talked to him before I went on my little retreat. No change in him at all?"

"*Nee*," Timothy groaned. "But all things are possible with God. We can pray, *jah?*"

My mind was cranking already about how our reconciliation meeting with Asa might end in him being a changed man....

Chapter 11

Timothy came down with an awful spring cold, or he was allergic to something growing in these parts, because his energy level was at zero. So, I went alone over to Asa's to ask if he'd attend a reconciliation meeting with Bishop Dan. Upon entering the house that evening, I noticed a stranger sitting at the table. Or was it someone at *Gmay* I'd never met, yet? "Hello. I'm Ruth Miller."

There was tension in the air as he said his name was Noah Coblenz, Asa's son. He shot a look of disdain at his father but quickly bowed his head, as if in prayer.

"Is Ivy home?" I asked Asa.

Noah swooshed at the air. "She's over at Lena's. Ivy's a caged animal, just like my *mamm* was." He spat the words like venom. "But Ivy sticks up for herself and can visit the neighbors, so I guess some things have changed."

"I, ah, will come back later," I fumbled.

Asa tapped the table. "I think you can help us."

My mouth gaped. "Me?"

He offered no tea or coffee but settled across the table near his son and offered me a seat. "Noah came the whole way out here from Montana to say he forgives me for something I didn't do, and I'm mighty mad. Haven't seen him in decades."

Noah pursed his lips and jutted is bearded jaw. "I held bitterness in my heart all these years. My *daed* treated my *mamm* badly. He refused medical care that could have saved her life."

"That's a lie!" Asa boomed.

"*Daed*, us three boys were married and out of the house or we would have done something. We didn't know, or we'd have called for help."

Before Asa could defend himself again, I spoke up. "What order of Amish are you in Montana? Real strict, not allowing too much medicine or modern ways? I used to be *Swartzentruber* Amish"

Noah's eyes blinked in disbelief. "Never met anyone who lived like them. We're definitely not like them, so backwards and all."

I wanted to correct Noah for his critical remark. There were still many fine folks up in Falcon Hill.

"He wants to blame me for his wife up and leaving him," Asa said softly. He clamped a hand on Noah's shoulder. "I don't deserve that."

"You sure don't," I gasped. "How old are you, Noah?"

"Forty. But if I had a *daed* like my neighbor Jonah Zook, I would have had a better example."

"Don't compare me to Jonah Zook!" Asa's face tightened, his blood vessels showing.

"That's another thing. Once you up and left us with Ivy, you stopped writing when I told you Jonah was my new neighbor. Why?"

Asa was struck dumb and was as still as a rock.

"*Daed*, don't you have anything to say?" Noah screamed.

The screen door opened and in walked Ivy. "Tell him, Asa. It's time."

"Jonah has nothing to do with anything. I tried to be the best *daed* I knew how. I didn't cause your wife to leave. I've taken blame for plenty, but not your adult problems."

I agreed with Asa. Noah was too old to play the blame game, as old as Eden.

Ivy sat next to me and reached across the table, gently placing her hand on Noah's. "You hardly remember me…"

"I had my eye on you, and my *daed* knew it. When *Mamm* died, he wanted another slave, and somehow got you."

"Noah, your *daed* rescued me from being disgraced. I've been learning from our new neighbors that the truth sets you free. So, you'll have it. I got pregnant by Jonah Zook and he had no intention of marrying me. We were of marrying age, but he was a coward. He said he'd deny he was the *daed*. The bishop asked Asa to marry me. No one knew I was three months along."

"It's why we left the area," Asa said, as if reliving a dream. "We knew tongues would wag, and I didn't want to put Ivy through that. We found a home here in Pennsylvania."

"I'm sure the Bishop didn't have to twist your arm to marry someone as beautiful as Ivy," Noah said, his eyes on Ivy.

"So, Noah," I started, "you and Ivy are the same age. Did you go to the same grade school?"

"*Jah*, we did," Ivy said.

"Did you like her back then, Noah?"

He rolled his eyes. "*Jah*, who wouldn't? But I had to get in line, so many ahead. But when she shocked us all and married my *daed*, it was so embarrassing."

"To you, *jah*?" I asked. "Hurt your pride? A pretty girl you're hoping to court chooses your *daed* over you." I scratched my chin. "Now that I think of it, why didn't the bishop ask *you* to marry Ivy?"

"Because he's had a fearful temper since birth," Asa said. "And he did something that ruined his reputation." Asa shifted, looking mighty uncomfortable. "When he was sixteen, an *Englisher* set fire to an Amish barn. Noah found out who did it, and set their barn on fire, too. And we all know the Amish don't retaliate."

"*Daed*, I was sixteen."

"Well, it's why the bishop didn't ask you to marry Ivy. Such actions have consequences."

Noah pounded the table. "I was sixteen!"

"Don't you see by now how hard life can be?" Asa asked, a catch in his voice. "It's time to stop this… this…"

"Keeping a record of wrongs?" I asked. "Time to bear all things? Hope all things? Love never gives up. First Corinthians 13 is a mighty powerful passage to ponder."

Ivy jumped from the table and grabbed her Bible. She opened it to where the book marker was. "I've been pondering all this. Asa, too. Listen:

Love is patient and is kind; love doesn't envy. Love doesn't brag, is not proud, doesn't behave itself inappropriately, doesn't seek its own way, is not provoked, takes no account of evil; doesn't rejoice in unrighteousness, but rejoices with the truth; bears all things, believes all things, hopes all things, endures all things. Love never fails.

Asa's face softened. "We got neighbors who showed us what a real marriage is supposed to be."

"*Jah*, Lena's helped me speak up and Timothy and Ruth have helped you…"

Asa stared at Ivy with a special twinkle in his eyes.

I shook my head, trying to take all this in. I had no reason to have a reconciliation meeting with Asa. Everything became right as rain just about now.

~*~

I sat quietly at home over the next two days as a soft steady rain fell over all the freshly planted fields. But the tranquil setting did not steady my mind. I got little sleep after meeting Noah, and he was still next door, him and Asa talking things out. What a *boppli*; I wanted to shout at him. He was nine years older than me. At my age, I never once thought of blaming my parents for any of my problems, especially marital problems.

But when I told Timothy that Asa started to see loving marriages in us and Lena and Jacob, my heart leapt for joy. Asa was bitter and didn't see the love Ivy offered him. But this morning I saw them walk hand in hand to the buggy. And was there a skip in the step of Asa Coblenz?

An *Englisher* neighbor stopped in to inform us that flash flood warnings had been issued on television. Timothy and I really didn't know of anything that needed to be done. There was a pond above the hill and it would surely collect all the water. And we had enough provisions for at least three weeks.

I sat and knit blankets for my precious *bopplin*. *Jah*, two *bopplin* I was carrying, and starting to feel it. Leg cramps at night already? What would I do when I was full term? Stephen said I had water retention and I was taking herbal supplements and got some relief.

Serena made a pot of tea and joined me. I wanted to bridge the topic of her getting a full-time job, but she admitted her mind was elsewhere. "Flood waters have crested the roads. My parents went the whole way to Yoder's Antique Mall."

"For what?" I asked.

"*Mamm* told me *Daed* wanted to buy her something special. Weird, huh? I think he's just trying to stay away from Noah. What a crank."

"*Jah*, he is. Did Rose meet him?"

"Rose has wanted to come by and meet him, but my parents said no."

"Noah's mouth comes unhinged a bit too easily," I said, attacking my knitting with more vigor. "I think they're afraid he may say something rude. He just found out who Rose's *daed* is."

"What? Does he still live out in Montana? Rose wants to meet him!"

I forced a smile. "All in *gut* time. Noah's in a bad spot. His wife left him, so please don't bring it up for a while. I hear Noah's staying for a few weeks. Might be spending Easter with us."

Suddenly, Timothy burst into the house, not even taking his work boots off. *Ach*, the mud! But he looked startled yet fidgety. And then he burst into tears.

"What is it?" I asked.

Between sobs, he choked out that he needed us to try to remain calm. He feared for our *bopplin* and me being so upset. I thought of the flash flood warnings. "Is Lena all right?"

I didn't want Timothy to speak, so afraid of the answer.

Timothy knelt at Serena's feet. "It's your *daed*. He saved your *mamm's* life but risked his own. The current was just too strong. He's presumed dead."

I heard about Asa and Ivy, but everything seemed gurgled. "What did you say?"

"Asa is gone. He saved Ivy's life but got swept under."

"Where's my *mamm*?" Serena blurted as she started to shake from shock. "I need to see my *mamm*. And my *daed* is gone? He wasn't so mean as people think. He wasn't!" she screamed.

The poor girl was in shock. She needed to see her *mamm* alive. "Where is she?"

"The Mennonite Church opened up for free medical care for those with minor injuries. Some are in the hospital, but I don't know where Ivy is. The little bridge a mile down the road washed out and back roads are flooded. The police closed some roads but will be open tomorrow."

I hugged Serena, trying to lend comfort.

"Is she cut and bruised? Does she have broken bones? And did my *daed* suffer much before he died?" Serena gasped for air. "I loved him…deep down."

"He's only presumed dead. They can't find his body…" Timothy informed.

I'd heard of bodies being found thirty-some miles away. Was he washed into the Mahoning River? Surely, they're dragging nets there. *Ach, Lord, Asa was just coming around to seeing Ivy's goodness. They could have had a second chance. Serena could have, too. I'm not questioning Your ways, but I just don't understand!*

~*~

Early the next day the back roads were opened; downed trees, some outbuildings washed away, and debris spit up from the water was everywhere. I hoped our buggy wouldn't get stuck in the thick mud. Amish and English were out and about, neighbors helping each other. Many trucks were out cutting down large branches threatening to crash down onto the road. "We sure got spared," I told Timothy. "Lots of seeds got washed away. I'll need to replant, but it's early yet."

Serena burst into tears. "My *daed* can't."

"Your *mamm* does the kitchen garden and your *daed* didn't have fields plowed up. He was a buggy maker."

"*Ach*, I meant my *daed* can't grow. Grow as a Christian. Since we got new neighbors, I noticed how he'd get mad, but walked away as if sorry."

"Your *daed* had his troubles, but he had an ever-softening heart..." Timothy said with feeling.

"Jah," I agreed. "Trust me on that. And I'm sure your *mamm* will help you understand many things. Now, please try to relax so when you see your *mamm*, you'll be prepared." I took her hands. "Let's pray. *Father, we need you. Your Word says You're our ever-present help in times of trouble. You say many are the trials in this life, but You get us through them all. Please give Serena peace. Your peace that passes understanding. Be her refuge and her strength. Cover her with your feathers, shield her in this storm. Amen.*"

"Amen. That was a nice prayer. Sounded like the Bible."

"Lots of Psalms strung together. I read the Psalms so much. They help me pour out my emotions when I don't know what to say. If I'm feeling down in the mouth, I say, 'Why are you downcast, soul? Why are you so disturbed, Hope in God!' Or something like that."

"She talks to herself," Timothy leaned over, winking at Serena.

Serena offered a faint grin. "Does it work, Ruth?"

"*Jah*, and Timothy does it, too. When he gets up in the morning he says, 'This is the day the Lord has made, I will rejoice and be glad in it.' He says it before coffee when he's a grump, but it sets his mind to look for joy and gladness in the day."

"I never get up grumpy," Timothy said. "I'm just not my merry self until my second cup of coffee."

I nudged him. "Just teasing, love."

We went into town and I was surprised that this sunny day had dried up the roads and sidewalks. We pulled into the hospital, as the Mennonite Church said Ivy wasn't there.

"I think Rose is here," Serena sputtered. "She'll know what to say to *Mamm*."

"Your *daed's* body hasn't been found, is all Ivy needs to know for now."

Chapter 12

Rose and Serena sat on either side of Ivy. Poor Ivy. Her arm was in a sling and her face was bruised and cut. "How are your legs?" Rose asked.

Ivy just stared, not speaking. Stephen was soon with us, and asked if we could all talk in private. The girls told Ivy they'd be right back, but Ivy said nothing. We went into a waiting room not far away and took our seats. I gripped Timothy's hand tight. He offered me a few squeezes, our signal that we could get through anything together, side by side.

Stephen faced the girls. "Your mother keeps asking for Asa. I thought I'd leave it up to the family members to break such bad news."

"He's only presumed dead," Timothy said. "It's not official."

"If they haven't found the body, rescue crews are out dragging the rivers. It rained all night on top of it all. I'd say it's safe to say he's gone."

"How's my mom?" Rose blurted out. "Are her legs okay? She's not moving them."

"Her legs are fine. Her arm is sprained. Now, her brain took a shaking. Imagine your head being tossed back and forth. The brain has room to move and gets banged up. But, thank God, no bleeding on the brain. It's a miracle, but she only has a mild concussion. But not one broken bone."

"I'll tell her *Daed* is gone, if you don't think it's too early," Rose offered.

"Well, I'd give her time to rest, but she won't stop asking for him. It's best that she knows the truth." Stephen gripped his clipboard. "There's something else. She has pneumonia and is on drip IV medicines and is a bit confused."

"I think we should tell her Asa's fine," Timothy exclaimed. "If I lost Ruth and was sick, it would do me in. A crushed spirit can't bear bad news. That's in the Bible somewhere."

"You're right," I said. "We're just…putting off the news for the right time, *jah*?"

~*~

Being at the hospital all day yesterday, I decided to stay home and cook up some meals for families who lost loved ones. Three from our *Gmay* were declared dead. *So unfathomable.* Their bodies would be embalmed and then set out in their houses for viewings, as was the Amish way. Many would stay at the houses around the clock and sit and pray. Just knowing someone was there was a great comfort. The only victim I got to know was Bill Weaver. His poor widow, dear Lillian, would have to raise her young family on her own for a while. I decided to make lots of cookies for the *kinner*.

There was still no word about Asa, so he was still presumed dead. Bishop Dan decided to not include him in the funeral two days away; he'd have his own when Ivy was well enough to attend and receive mourners. And who knew how long that would take? *Lord, have mercy on those girls. Rose seems the most distraught. It puzzles me to no end how odd she's been acting.* Never one to take things slowly, I decided right then and there to scoot on over to her house, seeing the church van in the driveway. I took one of the cookie trays over; maybe Rose needed some cheering up.

The blue sky seemed to mock us all. The chimney swifts darting around as if playing follow the leader, and then breaking away to play catch me if you can. The red winged black birds gave their two-toned song, which usually flooded me with peace, but not today. They irritated me. Was this grief? Two children dead. It wasn't fair.

I gave a quick rap on the Coblenz's screen door frame and yelled a cheery hello. Rose was at the sink and turned, telling me to come in, but her tone said, 'please go away.'

"I brought you some cookies. Thought they'd cheer you up some?"

Rose glared through me. "*Danki*, but nothing's going to cheer me up for a long time." She bit her lower lip. "I'm a Christian and all, but I just want to scream!"

"I understand. It's part of the stages of grief, I believe."

"I'm not grieved at all. It's that *bruder* of mine. He told me all about my real *daed*." Rose stomped a foot. "Why did he do that?"

I slowly sat at the table. "What?"

"Noah lives next door to my real *daed* and says that he's so kind! It makes me want to go out and meet him. How stupid of Noah to tell me right in the middle of this whole crisis. I feel like I'm split in two!"

"*Ach*, Rose. That was poor judgment on Noah's part." I opened the cookies and pulled out a sand tart. "Here, come sit and eat. It helps sometimes."

Rose gave a short-lived smile and agreed to sit a spell with me.

"Sure am glad the Lord goes before us, preparing the way," I said.

"I don't know what that means."

I admired Rose's honesty. "Well, I love Psalm 23 and say it before my feet hit the ground in the morning. You never know what a day will bring, and it's nice to know we have the Good Shepherd to lead us and protect us. Raising sheep, I know they're timid, but when they got to know my voice, they come right up to me."

"I know what you're going to say. Stay calm and let God lead."

I nodded. "*Jah*, that's part of it. As the psalm goes on, it talks about the Valley of the Shadow of Death.

That's a real place King David led his sheep through. He would go before his flock in case any bears, lions, or other wild animals could hurt his flock. Remember how David killed a lion and bear while a shepherd?"

Rose's features softened.

"Well, the shepherd's rod was a weapon along with a sling shot. So, he went before the sheep to make sure they were safe. So, wherever we go in life, the Lord has already been there and making sure we'll be okay."

"That's awesome!" Rose gasped and then covered her face as she let the tears flow. "I want to meet my *daed*."

"Of course, you do. That's natural, and maybe in *gut* time you will. But your *mamm* needs you here." Rose had uncovered too many secrets in a few months. She was illegitimate and now to find out her natural *daed* was kind. A kind Amish man. My mind started to churn. If this man was all that Noah said he was, would he be able to persuade Rose to return to the Amish?

"I told my pastor, you know. He thinks I need closure and should at least write to him. What do you think?"

I bit into a cookie. "I'd write. Can't hurt anything, right?"

Rose flushed. "I was thinking the same thing. What can one little letter do? Ruth, how do you do it?"

"Do what?"

"Get me to open up?"

Feeling strangely shy, I blushed. "I'm the one who barged over here."

"I'm glad you did, because I need your advice. Levi's two little cousins died in the flood and it's shaken his faith. He's talking like an atheist. And I have my hopes…"

It was obvious she was falling for this young Amish man.

"Could you talk to him? You and Timothy? He won't read his Bible, but scriptures ooze out of you."

Again, I felt shy, too much praise given. "You make me feel like a jelly filled donut. Ooze?" I laughed. "So, I'm looking as round as a donut. *Danki*, Rose!"

~*~

My green embroidered handkerchief got good use the day the Hostetler *kinner* were buried. Suzanna was my age, but looked so old and frail, not the robust woman she was. She leaned against Joe, her husband, who seemed to be spotting her lest she faint. Levi and his family looked much the same. Levi's face was set like flint. Was he angry? Or was he trying to keep himself together?

The dark storm clouds rumbled in the distance. Did we need a reminder of how the *kinner* were stolen? In a downpour? *Ach, Lord, why am I so angry!* I snapped at Timothy this morning for not putting his coffee mug in the sink. *Timothy never puts his coffee mug in the sink!*

Bishop Dan shook as he brought his message to an end. Oddly, he looked my way, as if needing my approval to continue. Confounded, I gave a simple nod.

"My dear flock, as we lay to rest Billy and James Hostetler, let us think of things eternal. In the Gospel of John it says, 'In the beginning was the Word, and the Word was with God, and the Word was God.' That means when all else shifts like sand in our lives, we have something to cling to that's eternal, the Bible. I want to encourage you all to read it daily, and if you have questions, come to me or one of the elders. Or go to someone older than you, like the Good Book says, the older teaching the younger." He held the Bible above his head. "I've found new strength in this book lately. Maybe God was preparing me, changing me, so I can help my flock in such great need."

He then led the crowd in silent prayer, but my mind was all but silent. I wanted to shout 'Hallelujah!' God did indeed lead me to this place where I could feel free to teach God's Word. *Ach, how precious is your Word, Lord, sweeter than honeycomb. I long to instruct the younger women and learn from the older.*

When I opened my eyes, my gaze met Stephen's and then Sarah's. They were glowing. They understood Bishop Dan's new found need for God's Word, not only for his life, but for the entire *Gmay*. I sighed. How I wished Ex-Amish could attend more than just funerals.

All was quiet except the wind whipping up. Flowers were thrown into the grave and then several men buried the coffin. Suzanna's scream pierced many hearts. Joe held her back as she got down on her knees and clawed at dirt that separated her from her *kinner*. Levi set his shovel down and placed a hand on Joe's shoulder. As the rain fell, he looked up in defiance towards God.

Lena had read a book on the stages of grief, but Stephen was here and welcome to stay for a little while. I took Timothy's hand and we met Stephen and Sarah under one of the massive porches. "Hello. Sad day, *jah?*"

"Sure is," Sarah said. "I feel so for Suzanna... We were close, and I want to comfort her, but...being Ex-Amish..."

I rubbed Sarah's back for a minute and then turned to Stephen. "I need help."

Timothy gasped. "Are you having contractions?"

I shook my head. "It's about grief. Aren't there stages people go through? One being anger?"

He nodded. "Yes, and anger can't be ignored. When women are sad they cry more easily than men. Men don't get sad, but mad."

"You seem like you're concerned about someone," Sarah said. "We have grief counseling over at the church."

"Someone asked us to talk to Levi," I said. "He's refusing to read his Bible and I hear he's losing his faith."

"That's normal," Stephen said. "He needs time. Levi was in a side field when the water rushed down and took the boys. He witnessed the whole tragedy."

"*Ach*, really?" Timothy said, blinking back tears. "So, do you think there's any hope of Asa turning up?"

Stephen leaned over. "No. It would be a miracle. One thing we can say is he's lived here long enough to see flooding and he knew what he was getting into. He must have jumped out of the buggy to drag Ivy to safety and then attempt to save his horse."

No greater love than someone dying for a friend, I pondered, this scripture running through my head.

Karen Anna Vogel

Chapter 13

It was with a heavy heart that we celebrated Easter Sunday. After communion and members paired up to wash feet, I pondered the whole way home why I still believed Asa was alive. I leaned my head against Timothy's shoulder as I inhaled the scent of apple blossoms as we rounded the bend to pass the apple orchard. What a site, white flowers bursting for acres.

"You're quiet. Tired?" Timothy asked.

"*Jah*, I suppose I am. Missed Asa today and with Ivy still in the hospital, it's not the Resurrection Sunday I'd envisioned."

"Envisioned?"

"I imagined I'd be washing Ivy's feet as well…"

Timothy slowed the horses pace. "Ivy will come home soon. I heard talk that she'll not be lacking in care, so many of the People going over to help her."

"Hope they crowd out Noah," I spat. "Wish he'd leave. Upsets Rose and Serena, and plants thoughts in their heads that Asa was a monster back in Montana. Did you believe his story that Asa wanted to leave Montana? To come to a place where his reputation wasn't tainted?"

"*Nee*, I did not," Timothy grumbled. "I look at fruit. Noah's wife left him for an *Englisher*. And something else, but I don't know if I should say it out loud."

My Timothy measured his words, so I knew this was serious indeed. "You can tell me. We can do some investigating."

He harrumphed. "Investigating? Still reading mysteries?"

"*Nee*, but one of Jane Austen's books, *Northanger Abbey*, has a mystery in it. A man is accused of killing his wife, but he didn't, just wore her out, snuffing out her spirit."

"You act like they're real people."

"Well, you can learn a thing or two about human nature. I was surprised when I read it that Asa didn't come to mind. When we first met, I thought he was snuffing the life out of Ivy, but not now. I think of Noah; isn't that odd?"

Timothy bit his lower lip. "They say the more you're married, the more you think alike." Then after a moment, he said, "Okay, I'll tell you what's been gnawing at me, but don't tell a soul. Don't chide me if you think it's ridiculous."

I laced my fingers through his. "Never."

"I don't like the way Noah looks at Ivy. And with Asa dead…"

This was a bit much. Noah couldn't remarry, his wife still being alive. But I encouraged Timothy to continue. Sometimes the smallest clue solved a mystery.

"Despite my disapproval of Asa in many ways, I spent hours trying to build him up. He had a strong root of rejection in him. He made a remark that struck me dumb. He quoted the scripture about if your mother and father forsook you, God never would. Made me think he had a hard childhood."

"We have to find out," I sputtered.

"Too late for that. Asa's gone."

"I don't believe it. I think there was foul play involved."

Timothy turned off a back road, not heading straight home. He wanted to talk. "Now, honey, you're pregnant and more emotional. Please, try to calm down. Foul play? There were eyewitnesses that he was swept away along with his horse."

"Did they find the horse's body?"

"*Ach*, Ruth. What are you thinking?"

"I don't know," I exclaimed. "When Noah came, Asa's state of mind took a nose dive. He was more protective of Ivy."

"Well, I'll tell you what I've been thinking. With Asa dead, for sure, I wouldn't put it past Noah to try to lure her…"

"We need to find Asa!" I said confidently. "The river runs south towards Smicksburg. Maybe we could go down and do some investigating."

"That's *ferhoodled*, Ruth." He elbowed me. "You were fonder of Asa than you let on, *jah*? Grieving his death?"

I swallowed the lump in my throat. "*Jah.*"

~*~

I decided to rest for a week, knowing I'd been pushing myself too much, emotionally and physically. I got a chance to visit with Jacob's parents when they came from Falcon Hill to visit. Oddly, Samuel asked many questions about fishing. He'd read that Pittsburgh had more bridges than any place in the world. That meant rivers and lots of fish. He also knew there were new Amish settlements popping up in Western Pennsylvania. Puzzled, I pulled Martha aside to ask her if he was thinking of fishing for a living, and she said he's thinking outside the box. What did that mean? Martha offered me a comical grin, as if to thank me for opening their minds to other occupations besides farming. I was just glad to see Jacob feeling the approval of his parents for being a carpenter. And their coming made a loud statement to folks in Falcon Hill and I hoped Becky would wake up and write Lena.

On this fine Lord's Day, Ivy came home, miraculously well enough to talk lucidly. Timothy wanted me all to himself and we sat around the table, putting a new puzzle together. I never got tired of this man's company. I always said Lena was my best friend, but that was after Timothy. I cringe still to this day to think I could have been hastily married to someone else. This man loved me so tenderly. So concerned lately about my nerves, he let one of the cats in the house. A gentle creature whose purr soothed me. The orange tabby rested in my lap now, my protruding belling making little space.

All was so peaceful until someone pounded on the door. Must be the *Englisher* neighbor down the road. Amish didn't pound unless there was a fire or emergency. The English thought since we didn't have doorbells, we needed loud banging.

But I heard Noah's voice. I picked up the kitty and nestled my face in her fur. This day was going so well. When Timothy ushered Noah through the utility room into the kitchen, I was not prepared for what came next. Noah sobbing? What on earth?

"Read this," Noah said, handing a letter to Timothy.

"From back home? But there's no mail today."

Noah took a seat. "I forgot to get it yesterday. Bad news."

Timothy readjusted his wire-rimmed glasses and read:

Noah,

I'm writing to let you know that your wife is dead.

Bishop Jonah

"I'm sorry, Noah," Timothy said.

I only nodded, not able to bear Noah's hypocrisy. "Such a short note for such a serious matter. Your bishop is a man of few words?"

"*Jah*, very few."

"What's your wife's name?" Timothy oddly asked.

"Mary Coblenz."

"You should write something up for the Budget, saying something nice about your wife. And to inform the People across the country."

"I'm not *gut* with words." He swiped away a tear. "And cancer is a horrible thing. She shrank down to skin and bones."

Timothy near collapsed in a chair. "Your wife had cancer? You said she ran off with an *Englisher*."

"She d-did!" He cracked a few knuckles. "There was an *Englisher* who took a shining to Mary. Real rich man who accused me of not getting Mary help. Mary went off with him to a cancer treatment place to live."

"Noah! Is there no end to your deceit?" Timothy boomed. "You accused Asa of treating your *mamm* and Ivy bad, but you left your wife to die alone?"

"The center has staff. Anyhow, I'm sure Liam McKensey was by her side. He loved her."

I stared aimlessly at Timothy, speechless.

Timothy's face contorted, and he clenched his fist. "You're one mysterious man, Noah."

Noah sprang to his feet. "I came over here for comfort, and all I get is judgment. You're so Amish!"

"And you're not?" I prodded. "Noah, when you feel like you can be truthful about your past, we're here to help in any way, but your words contradict."

He swiped the air. "Ivy understands me."

"She's too sick to help you," Timothy snapped. "And folks plan to come over to help. Maybe it's time you left. Go home to your wife's funeral."

Noah glared at Timothy and then me. "I'm staying. It's my *daed's* house."

~*~

Ivy looked much better than I expected, although too pale for my liking. Bed rest was ordered along with many pills. Stephen said Ivy needed supplements and he was going tomorrow to see Reed Byler, the herbalist in Smicksburg. I dreamt last night I was running around the streets of Smicksburg trying to find Asa, and I did. I needed an herb for my nerves!

I sat at the end of Ivy's bed and reached for her hand. "We'll get you right as rain in no time."

"Find Asa," she begged. "He's a *gut* swimmer. He didn't drown."

I blinked back tears. Ivy really cared for her husband. She'd seen his soft side like I recently had. "You'll see him again." I pointed to the heavens.

"Please, Ruth. Have the men search. Tell Timothy."

"Ivy, do you realize how long the men have been looking? I don't want to upset you, but maybe you don't know. The rivers were dragged."

Ivy motioned for me to shut her bedroom door. "I'm so afraid of Noah. There's something sinister about him."

"His wife died of cancer, did you know that? He told us she left him, all the while a nice *Englisher* took her to a cancer treatment center. That's fudging your words. *Jah*, she left, but not in a romantic way." I massaged my temples. "He came over yesterday with a short one line note from his bishop, saying his wife was dead."

Ivy huddled, as if to protect herself. "He wrote that letter is what. He said his wife died before Easter and how she was spending Resurrection Sunday in heaven. I could write back home to Montana and find out."

I hushed her as her face was now white as snow. "You rest. I'll get to the bottom of this."

"*Ach*, too weak to think. Rose will take care of it. She'll be gone a few days. Lots of help coming from the People, I told her it was okay."

"To do what?"

"Fly out to Montana to meet her *daed*. Needs to hear back from the bishop in the settlement first. She'll need a place to stay."

This strangely warmed my heart yet sent a chill down my spine. The People had shown care towards Ivy like she'd never experienced. But what would Rose find in Montana?

~*~

Levi stopped over that night, admitting that Rose had sent him. Timothy teased that Eva Angel could answer any doubts he had about his faith, which touched me deeply, but Levi looked stunned. "My faith? My faith has never been more solid. Pouring over scripture and seeing the sovereignty of God. It's brought me to my knees at night when I pray. *Jah*, I saw the boys be taken to glory, I see the heartache of all who loved them, but I've never known deep down God…holds all things together in His hands."

"Beautiful," I couldn't help but exclaim. "That's a hard thing to get into the heart."

"*Jah*, and it was one of the reasons I didn't get baptized some five years ago. The Amish really believe everything is sifted through God's hands before it can happen. I bucked against that, since it made me feel helpless. Truth is, I thought God was mean, but now I know He is love."

Timothy cleared his throat. "And how did you discover God is love?"

"At New Life Church. I know you don't like me saying that, but it's the truth."

"So, you'll be going to that church then? Leave the People?"

He shook his head vehemently. "With all the changes with the bishop, allowing Bible reading, not being so uptight if we mix with Mennonites, I find it the perfect fit. And I believe I have you two to thank, being bold enough to speak the truth in love."

Bold. That was one characteristic I didn't like to be accused of, but Levi admired it. I suppose the Bible did say to be bold, courageous. I slipped a glance at Timothy, who was trying to hide a smile, or was it pride in a good way?

"So, Levi," I said, "Rose's concerns about your faith are unfounded."

"*Jah*, for sure, but I did want to get your advice about Rose. You see, I love that girl, but can't go to her church. My roots are in the Amish and a slow-paced life. All the modern gadgets she has makes me nervous. Seems so unnatural. But, we've admitted we care for each other."

"Enough to get married then, or we wouldn't be talking about your differences," Timothy observed. "Do you think Rose would come back to the People? She thinks we're mighty backwards."

Levi slipped his hands up and down his suspenders. "She's hurt. Not respectable talking about the dead, but Asa turned her from the Amish so much, it would take a miracle for her to be baptized."

Needing comfort, I picked up my knitting needles and yarn. "We got to know the real Asa. Sure do wish Rose could have seen his tender side."

"That's what I tell her. He taught me how to pitch."

"Pitch manure? Didn't your own *daed* teach you that?" Timothy asked.

Levi let out a hearty laugh. "Pitch a baseball!"

We all chuckled, and Timothy explained that we weren't allowed to play baseball in Falcon Hill.

"He taught me a curve ball. Sometimes he'd have Rose and Serena watch the kids play ball from the buggy. Why they weren't allowed to play, Rose could never figure out. That her *mamm* lived like a hermit was a scary thing to us *kinner*. Some thought she had some contagious disease, but we all know now why. The People would have forgiven Ivy's past sin and welcomed their family into the community."

"They've been doing that in abundance since they found out and now the pouring out of love towards Ivy is heartwarming," I said.

"I've pointed all this out to Rose, and I think it's affecting her, but she said she'd never be Amish," Levi groaned hopelessly.

"Pray," Timothy said. "God has a plan. If you two are meant to be husband and wife, God will work it out. Like you said, he's a loving God, *jah*? He has a plan." He set his eyes on me. "He gave me Ruth, something I thought was impossible. She turned down so many proposals, it took me months to get up the courage to ask."

"*Ach*, Timothy, you know why." I hid my face behind the bundle of yarn, blushing to beat the band.

"*Jah*, you were too independent."

"I was not. All the men who asked wanted to change and control me."

Levi clapped his hands. "That's what Rose says. You thought that, too?"

"I knew it. But Timothy was patient and kind. I didn't fear him, and his love made me not afraid. Timothy brings out the best in me, even though he's a tease at times."

"Love is patient and kind, like the Bible says," Levi said solemnly. "I've been trying to discourage Rose from flying out to meet her *daed*. Afraid she'll get hurt, or maybe stay in Montana. I need to be patient. I need to encourage her."

I tried to absorb all that Levi was saying. Did I, Eva Angel, along with Stephen and the Mennonites, turn this whole community towards God, reading his Word? Praise be!

Chapter 14

Ach, the joy of being in my garden, so lush this year, due to all the rain. Rain. It was a blessing and a curse. Broke open my seeds to hatch new life but snatched Asa's. How the man was growing on me, seeing his tender side few saw. Gossip abounded in hushed circles that Ivy was set free from a burdensome husband. Serena overheard such nonsense and outright rebuked them to their faces. What spunk that girl showed. As timid as a mouse when I met her but now she pounced like a hungry cat. Maybe it was grief, but if I felt gypped on knowing the kind side of Asa, I'm sure Serena felt it more.

I sipped my coffee, waiting for Lena to arrive for our little prayer time, watching the sun rise over the rolling hills. *Ach, Lord, you're so beautiful. The heavens declare your glory. You make all things new. The dew each morning refreshing the earth. Please, bring refreshment to Ivy and her girls. They seem mighty parched.* My eye caught Lena strolling over from her place and Rose running from hers. What on earth? When they met, Rose sunk into Lena's embrace. I tried to soak this in. Lena had run to me for comfort many a time, and now others were running to her. Lena was strong being married to Jacob.

Lena and Rose locked arms and walked my way. Upon seeing me, Rose ran to me for a hug. "He said no!" Rose cried out, now wailing.

I rubbed her back and tried to calm her. "Who said no?"

"The bishop out there in Montana. His name is Ichabod. Ugly name. How appropriate."

Lena and I led her inside and to my long bench. "What reasons did he give? I'm sure there were reasons."

Rose yanked out a letter. "Read this. *Ach*, who is he to say I can't meet my real *daed*!"

I took the letter and read aloud:

Rose,

First, let me say I'm sorry to hear of Asa's death. He was a good man. A close friend.

You're right in saying Jonah Zook is your real daed, but Asa adopted you. You weren't supposed to know, and I can't be a part of something not natural. You see, Jonah has a family of his own. If you visit, it may upset the apple cart. What's in the past is in the past.

You say Asa never loved you. We've written for years now and he's said some mighty loving things about you. Let things be as they are and let nature take its course. Regrets over the past rob us of the present. Right now, your mamm needs you.

I hope to meet you at the funeral if our arrangements get worked out.

I'll be praying for you,

Ichabod

I sat a while before speaking, as did Lena. The two-toned song of the red winged blackbird soothed me. Only two tones. How simple. If life could only be two clear choices, but it never was.

"I'd take that as God's answer to you," Lena said. "Sometimes life is confusing, and we feel like we're on a raging river. Look for the next stone to cross that river." She leaned over, gazing at me ever so tenderly. "Ruth taught me that when I was in quite a storm."

Rose slouched. "But I want to meet my real father. I need closure. We all need closure, right?"

"Closure?" Lena asked. "What do you mean?"

"Well, I've taken psychology classes in college and closure, well, it answers questions. Gives us reasons why things happen."

"What?" Lena gasped. "We'll never understand everything this side of eternity. We look through a dark glass now. When we get to heaven, we'll get our so-called closure, but for now we walk by faith. God never told Job why he lost his *kinner*, livestock, health, and left him with a crabby wife."

"It was Satan who stole everything from Job," Rose informed.

I cleared my throat. "We know that, but Job never did. He held on to his faith in a loving God." I took Rose's hand. "Can you do that?"

Lena took the other. "You know how I struggle that I'm estranged from my sister, *jah*? That I lost both parents when I was ten? I'd go mad trying to figure everything out. *Nee*, I trust God."

Rose lowered her pretty head and let the tears drip onto her gray tee-shirt. "The Amish have such a peace that everything will be okay. Why can't I?"

Lena and I knew Rose was going through the grieving process and just sat and mourned with her. Obviously, she was torn. *Lord, help my neighbors. As spring unfolds around us, blossoms exuding fragrance, help them through these rough times. A crushed flower gives off perfume. They're crushed. Bear them up for the funeral. Help the Coblenz women see the love of community coming together to show their love. Help them receive it, something only a humble heart can receive. Soften Rose's heart.*

~*~

Timothy wouldn't let me carry more than one pie over to Ivy's the day of the funeral. Mighty concerned he was about me as my middle was expanding rapidly. *Bless my twins, Lord.* Buggies lined up evenly up and down the road, along with cars from English friends and Ex-Amish, as they were welcome to funerals. Lena and Jacob met us at the side door, concern etched onto their faces. "What is it?" I asked.

"There're Amish here from Montana." Lena pointed to a few vans parked up the road. "And Noah took off. Not here for his own *daed's* funeral."

Timothy squeezed my shoulder, his signal for me not to get involved. "Let's be fully present to help Ivy and the girls and forget about Noah. The truth about him will come out."

"The truth?" Jacob asked. "You suspect him not being Amish, too?"

I cocked my head back like a mean rooster. "You think that?"

"*Jah*. He came over to my new shop and slipped a few times. Squirrely man for sure."

"The truth will come out," Timothy insisted, ushering me into the house.

Of all times to be so big! I could scarcely get through to the tables set up for the meal. To say I was bushed making pulled pork and roast beef with other women from the *Gmay* was an understatement. The four of us made our way to the front to sit next to Ivy and the girls.

Rose glared at me and switched seats with Serena to sit next to me. "What have I done?" I whispered.

"Nothing. I'm so nervous. The bishop from Montana is here! And I'm so angry with him not letting me go out. *Mamm's* so nervous, too, that her secret, namely me, the *illegitimate* child, will get out to them, since folks here know about it."

I gripped her hands. "No one is illegitimate in God's eyes. He knew you in your *mamm's* womb. He knit you together, fashioned you. And He did a *gut* job. You're lovely inside and out."

"*Danki*, Ruth. You always say the right things."

As the room kept swelling with mourners, I wondered if we should have let Ivy use our barn. Soon we'd need to open windows as some would have to stand outside. Well, there was no body to view, no filing through to give last respects to the deceased, so the house wouldn't get too congested.

I looked back and saw Levi, who motioned for me to come to him. *Ach*, I'm carrying twins, so I motioned for him to come to me, and he did. "What is it?" I asked.

He cupped his hands and whispered, "Can I sit next to Rose?"

Timothy must have overheard and got up to stand against the wall, making room on the bench for Levi. I tried not to listen to Levi speak tenderly to Rose, encouraging her, lifting her slumped shoulders. These two were meant to be together, it was clear. We'd just have to keep praying Rose could see Amish men as not so domineering.

~*~

After the service and the meal was shared, a tall, lanky, elderly man introduced himself. "I'm Bishop Ichabod from Montana. Rose pointed you out as being neighbors and *gut* friends."

"Nice to meet you," Timothy said, offering him the right hand of fellowship with a kiss on the cheek.

"I want to talk to Rose, but she wants you there, along with her friend, Levi. Can we go to your house for a talk?"

"*Jah*, sure," Timothy said, but I wanted to protest. My house was usually spotless but with all the preparations for today, I left my mop and broom right in the middle of the living room. And dishes in the sink! Timothy grabbed my hand as we walked to the house, telling me he'd run in and *redd* things up while I showed the bishop the grafted apple tree. *Ach*, I loved my husband!

So, he sped up and I showed the bishop how four different types of apples grew from the same tree, some Granny Smith green ones and all the others different shades of red. He was amazed and said he'd be using it as an example for a future sermon. He noticed my kitchen garden overflowing with herbs and lettuces of so many varieties, he put his hands on his hips and just stared, saying I had a green thumb for sure and certain.

Timothy came out of the house. "*Yinz* all coming in?" He asked, a smile landing on me.

"*Yinz*. I've heard that quite a bit," the bishop said with a chuckle. "When I travel down to Texas to visit kin, they say *y'all*, but I've never heard *yens*."

I decided not to correct his pronunciation as we entered the house. Rose was so pale it was pitiful, but Levi held her hand. Praise be!

The circle of rockers and benches were filled, and Bishop Ichabod asked if we could have silent prayer, which we did. He cleared his throat and bit his lower lip, stalling. "I'll try to be brief, since we're headed back to Montana tonight. I need to reveal some unpleasant information. First, Noah only came out here for money. He left the Amish years ago. I confronted him. He said he was taking the vow, but I don't believe him. What he wanted was money and to blame Asa for ruining his life. But he wanted money more than anything. Now, with Asa gone, I suspect he wants an inheritance, but the house is in Asa and Ivy's name. Warn Ivy, when the time is right."

"*Danki* for sharing that with us," Timothy said. "We'll be watching over Ivy and the girls."

The bishop nodded thanks. He pulled a thick envelope out of his vest and handed it to Rose. "I think these are yours. Asa and I wrote often, and he spoke of you with great love, just not able to express it. I cut out parts of the letter meant only for me, so what you have looks like Swiss cheese."

Rose took the envelope, but anger was etched into her brow. "He hated me, but thank you for trying."

The bishop knelt before Rose. "Asa never had much confidence. He always said such a beautiful woman like Ivy could never love him. And seeing you, he was sure she'd always love your *daed*. He was a vexed man, until your new neighbors moved in."

He rose and faced me. "Asa wrote about his so-called outspoken new Amish neighbor named Ruth. *Ach*, how you got under his skin in a *gut* way. The Lord used you to see our Lord and Savior. The more he irked you, you extended grace. Unconditional love. It changed him. And Timothy's love for you showed him how a wife should be treated. I'm so grateful for you both."

He handed a slim envelope to Timothy. "He explains it all in his last letter."

Taking a seat, he asked if we had any questions. Rose was quick to ask what her real father was like.

"He has a large farm with ten *kinner.*"

"So, I have ten stepbrothers and sisters?" Rose asked.

"Rose, I'm so sorry to tell you, but Jonas doesn't want his wife to know about you. She's suffered from MS for years and he believes if she knew about you, it would set her back."

Rose held her middle as if in pain. "He could meet me in secret. He's a coward."

"He is a coward," the bishop said. "He wouldn't marry your *mamm.* They were courting, but his love for money blinded him. He said he wasn't ready financially and gave Ivy up, along with you. When I asked Asa to marry your *mamm,* he stepped forward, but Ivy wasn't too keen on it, and she said some things to Asa that cut him to the heart. Some words you don't get over…"

"Such as?" Rose challenged.

"That he'd never hold a candle up to Jonah. Asa knew he needed to leave the community or Ivy would never get over Jonah. And from what Asa wrote, she did show affection and realized Jonah never loved her."

"I heard her say that," I said.

"So, Rose, you read those letters, let the truth set you free. *Jah*, Asa was a vexed man, always missing Montana, always afraid Ivy would feel shame. And do you know why?"

Rose shrugged her shoulders rather rudely.

"He was illegitimate himself. He wanted to protect you, but I think it all came across as being controlling. He carried so much shame, it was pitiful."

Rose slowly looked up, eyes tender. "He always yelled at me for slouching. Act proud, not ashamed of yourself. So, I walked with a book on my head for years." Her chin quivered as tears filled her eyes. "He was trying to protect me from the shame he felt? He projected his emotions onto me?"

"Well, that I don't know. About the projecting part," the bishop confessed.

"It's done by hurting people. He felt shame but wouldn't deal with it, so projected it on to me. I can see he did it to my *mamm*, too. He wasn't protecting her from shame, but himself."

The bishop rearranged his straw hat. "Well, that's hard to comprehend, but if it helps you understand Asa, that's a *gut* thing."

"I studied psychology in college. *Danki* for the letters and all this information. Can I write to you if I have more questions?"

The bishop's smile lit up the room. "Of course." He shook hands with everyone before leaving. Levi held Rose in his arms as she wept, letting out years of emotions.

Chapter 15

Ever the curious one, I begged Timothy to not rush back over to Ivy's but read what was in the envelope. "Asa wrote about us? Hard to believe."

"*Jah*," Timothy agreed, tearing open the letter. We sat snuggly on the bench, reading it silently together.

Ichabod,

Remember that woman that got under my skin? That new neighbor I wrote about? Well, there was a reason I didn't like her. When I irritated her, she was usually pretty nice. And even when I reported her to the bishop about the Glory Barn and having a cellphone in the barn, she seemed to pity me. It was like she could see through me.

I think sometimes God uses people, since we can't see God. Well, at least that's how it happened to me. After one of my rants, Ruth called me a hypocrite. An actor. She said it with such concern, and I knew she was right. I took a walk and cried my eyes out. Asked God to change me. Talked to God like he was my real father, and I felt like God loved me for the first time.

Let me back up. Timothy, Ruth's husband, has been a real nice neighbor. Very patient man. Loves his wife like a man should. Never really saw a marriage like theirs. My other new neighbors have the same nice marriage, too. Well, we became friends and spent time together. So, they all helped me see God.

God became so real to me through these folks, like I said, I cried like a baby one night. And then I did what Ivy told me many times. Repent and ask for God's forgiveness. Just God and me. Not me and the bishop but just admitting to God my heart needed a good scrubbing. I've only told Ivy this, but I felt clean for the first time in my life. As the days went by, love for Ivy and my girls grew. My hard heart was taken out and a soft one put in, like the Bible says. A new heart will I give you, a new spirit will I put in you. That's in the Bible in Ezekiel. It happened to me.

I feel like I've been born from above, like Jesus said we must to enter the kingdom of God. I know this was supposed to happen to me at baptism, but it didn't. Can't explain why. Nothing wrong with the People we grew up with, it was me. You know my struggles. I think I've always felt unworthy. Well, my new neighbors helped me see the love of God and I'm thankful. Need to tell them this, but headed out to take Ivy shopping for something she's wanted for a long time. A spinning wheel. The neighbor women knit, and Ivy learned. I'll spend the rest of my life trying to do all I can to make that woman happy.

Write back soon,

Asa

I grabbed a handkerchief from my sleeve and cried for joy and sorrow. Love was a powerful thing. It changed Asa. And I never knew until now just how much I loved that man and missed him.

"We hardly did anything for him," Timothy said, his voice catching in his throat. "Let him tag along, went to Yoder's with him. Played games. Nothing big."

"I know. It's like my garden. Tiny little seeds started it."

"You're right, but I feel like we don't deserve all this praise," Timothy said with a sigh. "I miss Asa. He and Ivy could have had a whole new marriage."

I could only nod in agreement.

~*~

I hardly saw Timothy for three days straight as he insisted I keep my legs up. I didn't protest, since Lena and

I helped the most with the funeral. And Lena was spending time with her precious little ones undisturbed. *Ach*, to see her restored was a joy. I knew it was no accident that now Lena was right by Ivy to help her adjust to widowhood.

Grabbing my yarn I'd spun weeks ago, I cast on forty-two stitches to make another blanket. My *bopplin* would be snug as a bug in a rug for sure. The tick tock of the pendulum clock soothed me. It gently reminded me that time goes on, ever so slowly. My eyes grew heavy and I would have dozed off completely if my cat wasn't so affectionate. When my hands dropped, it was her cue to sit on my lap.

"Ruth, can we talk?"

I near jumped out of my skin. "Ivy, I didn't hear you come in." I fanned my face with the knitting pattern. "Sure, come sit." Ivy was so soft-spoken, I hadn't heard. "I get so wrapped up in knitting, sometimes I'm in a world of my own."

Ivy lowered her gaze as she sat in the rocker across from me. "I miss Asa. Everything over there reminds me of him. Noah's been a great help."

Ach, Lord, help me break this most unpleasant news. "Has Timothy talked to you about Noah?"

"*Nee*. Why?"

I surmised Timothy was catching up here on our farm and hadn't had time yet. "Did Bishop Ichabod from Montana talk with you then, about Noah?"

Ivy pursed her lips. "*Nee*, he barely said two words to me. Still treats me like a sinful woman. Noah's right in wanting to come live under our *Gmay*."

"He what?" I exclaimed. "He's not leaving? Ivy, I need to tell you something. Noah's an awful liar. He left the Amish long ago. Bishop Ichabod told us all about him and said to warn you."

Ivy rested her head in her hands. "I have my suspicions. Some of his ways don't seem Amish. But he's repented and wants to be baptized. Did you know that?"

Now I needed my kitty on my lap for comfort, so I scooped her up. "Ivy, he wants money…and I see how he looks at you." A shiver raced down my spine. "He shouldn't be staying over at your place."

Ivy looked up at me in disbelief. "He's Asa's son. It's his home."

Now I wanted to pitch my yarn at Ivy, Lord forgive me. I wanted to scream, 'Wake up!' I measured my breathing, knowing what I had said probably shocked her. I was rattling on too fast. "What I can't get over is that Noah was never married, and he dressed Amish, begging folks for money to help his wife. So pathetic."

"She didn't die?" Ivy asked.

I hugged my yarn. "I think Bishop Dan should talk to you. I have other news not so glum. When you're feeling stronger, I want you to read a letter Asa wrote to Bishop Ichabod the day of…the accident." I forced a smile. "Did you know Asa was taking you out to get a spinning wheel?"

She held one hand to her throat. "Asa mentioned me?"

I smiled. "In the kindest way."

Ivy blinked in disbelief. "Asa said we were taking a drive to see the blossoms. We've never taken a leisurely ride to enjoy nature, but he said he knew of a cherry orchard he wanted me to see…" Ivy's eyes watered and then spilled over onto her thin face. She yanked a handkerchief out of her sleeve and pat her eyes. "I had such hopes."

"I'm so sorry, Ivy," was all I could say. What Ivy needed was a friend to sit by her, to mourn with her, not jabber on about things she could care less about right now. No one had said anything about Noah needing money just yet for good reasons; Ivy had no strength to confront him. *Learn from the dog, he wags his tail and not his tongue!* I chided myself. I'd tell Timothy and Bishop Dan to confront Noah when they saw fit.

~*~

After the noon meal, I put my feet back up and indulged myself in a day of knitting. But someone knocked on the front door. No one knocked on the front door except *Englishers*. I did love some of my new trusted English friends stopping over, especially members of my knitting circle. "Come on in," I yelled, glad the windows were up and I had a strong voice.

"Ruth, do you have time to talk?" Rose said, her face pinched.

"Sure, come in. Just following Timothy's orders to sit and knit." I grinned. "Remember when I met you at the Country Store and you thought Timothy ordered me around?"

"Yes, I do. My views are changing so fast on that matter." Rose took a seat and huffed. "Don't see men like I used to. Well, maybe most men. Noah's getting on my last nerve. He keeps saying Bishop Ichabod lied about him needing money and he wants to become Amish." She bowed her head and chewed her bottom lip. "But I read my *daed's* letters. Did something to me. I misjudged him."

I was pleased as punch to hear this. "We did, too. What he wrote Ichabod about us showed us that Asa carried lots of pain."

Rose leaned forward. "Exactly. Now I see he might have become my *daed* to spare me the shame he felt, being illegitimate. And he loved my *mamm*, too. Did you know that? *Mamm* confessed she was harsh to him at first, still being in love with my real *daed*." Rose fidgeted with her silver necklace and sighed.

"What else is on your mind?" I prodded, knowing she was holding back deep water.

"I'm afraid to say it out loud!"

"Is it bad?"

"*Nee*, it makes me feel…bad. For as long as I can remember, I've despised the Amish, but now I know why! My *daed* sheltered us all because of *Mamm's* secret. Me!

204

And I've been welcomed in with such love, I must say, I've never known such kindness at any English church. The People have given so much money to *Mamm*, locally and from other states. We even got some from Canada."

It was sad Rose was just being exposed to all the blessings the Amish poured out. "Now you need to go to a quilting frolic or my knitting circle and see how much bonding goes on around a craft."

"Old Anna May Yoder asked me to come to a quilting frolic at her tiny *dawdyhaus* and I said yes."

"*Gut!* One step at a time. You'll find the path you're supposed to be on. There's no rush, *jah*?"

"That's another thing," Rose said. "Levi is being so patient. He's going to take baptismal classes, so he'll be Amish for sure." She smiled. "I remember us signing up for classes when I was eighteen, but then he dropped out. I did, too. Never met a man I loved as much as Levi."

I let my yarn rest in my lap. "Wasn't Levi the town bad boy?"

Rose rolled her eyes. "During *Rumspringa* he drank a bit too much one night and came drunk to a Singing. It was all blown out of proportion by my parents. Now I see *Mamm* came down hard on Levi, always has, fearing I'll make the same mistake she did..."

"Have a child out of wedlock? *Ach*, Rose, I can see how you've been so confused. Your parents dumped lots of shame and fear on you."

Rose straightened and pointed heavenward. "God became my father in a powerful way. Through the Bible, I could see how loving he is. And so many scriptures like, 'If your mother and father despise you, I never will,' came alive. If it wasn't for the life-changing power in the Bible, and some counseling, I'd be really messed up, *jah*?"

"*Jah*." I beamed at this beautiful friend. She talked to me like a *mamm*, but I wasn't much older. "So, Levi isn't pressuring you to be Amish –"

"I want to be Amish," Rose blurted. "I'm just so afraid of making the decision. It's a vow like a marriage vow."

I was glad my decision to be Amish came quite easily. Rose had seen the world and all it offered. "We'll pray, and God will lead. Timothy had a farm book out and I wanted to know why my sheep get so skittish when it rains. Come to find out, they're afraid of the sound of running water. So, when the pond on the hill overflows a bit, even little rivulets, they huddle together, petrified. So, in Psalm 23, when King David says, 'He leadeth beside still waters,' it's for a reason. Want to know something else? Sheep can't digest their food until they lie down, so the shepherd forces them to lie down." I twinkled my toes. "Timothy read that part and that's why I'm here with my feet up." I reached over to Rose and she took my hand. "*Jah.* I've loved you and Serena since the day you yelled at us at the store."

"Stop teasing," Rose said with a laugh.

"Okay, I'll stop. What I want to say is you've taught me so much about what evangelicals believe. We're nearly the same age. Let's be friends and don't look at me like a mother figure." I poked my belly. "Even though it's the figure I have right now."

Rose's mouth gaped. "I've helped you? You asked questions and I answered them."

"And I think you've helped the whole *Gmay*."

"Shut up!" Rose cheered.

Shut up? I shrugged my shoulders and resumed knitting. Rose bellowed out a hardy laugh. "I don't mean shut up literally. It's slang for...I can't believe that."

"You can't believe what?" I asked, losing my train of thought.

"That I helped the *Gmay*!"

"Well, you did. All I learned from you I passed on to others and, well, it's all in the Bible. Bishop Dan being more lenient now, encouraging Bible reading…you had a part in it."

Rose stared in disbelief. "Wow, that's awesome."

I heard a siren and immediately shot up a prayer that no buggy was hit. Rose ran to the window. "There's a police car over at my place."

Chapter 16

Adrenaline flew through me, causing me to pick up my pace. Noah was resisting being handcuffed as two policemen tackled him to the ground. It was all too surreal. Three police cars lined the driveway, one parked along the road, while cops ran around the house, looking for something…or someone. "Officer!" I yelled as one seemed to be hurting Noah's arms. After they cuffed him, they yanked him up.

"Step back. This man is dangerous," an elderly officer commanded.

Ivy ran outside, pleading for them to leave Noah alone, but the police told Noah he had a right to get a lawyer and anything he said would be held against him. They shoved him into the police car while Noah kept spitting out profanities.

Ivy cupped her mouth. "Noah, what did you do?"

"Ma'am, check any valuables that may be missing," said the officer. "Others in the community may want to do the same."

Valuables? I wanted to scoff. The Amish have valuables? A man's life was valuable. "Officer, can I speak one minute to Noah?" I begged.

A tall burly officer stepped aside but warned me not to get too close. And he wanted to hear what I had to say. "Noah, there is no pit God can't get you out of. No matter what you've done, ask God to forgive you. You remember that, *jah?*"

Ivy began to scream at the police who flashed a search warrant in front of her and entered her house. "What are you looking for?"

"Drugs or others hiding out here from his gang."

Rose ran to prop up her *mamm* and being familiar with the English world spoke up. "Officer, I live in that house and I can assure you there's no one in there except my sister, who's going to be petrified out of her mind. As for drugs, I know what marijuana smells like. It makes me nauseated."

One young police officer seemed charmed by Rose. "Well, thank you, but that's not what we're looking for."

Rose held her throat. "Cocaine? Was he dealing something strong?"

Serena stormed out the door and marched over to us, arms crossed in protest. "*Mamm*, the police are dumping all our flour and sugar out."

"Cocaine," the officer said. "I hate to alarm you women, but did you know you were housing a wanted man? We'll have to question you."

"We're Amish!" Rose proclaimed. "We welcome anyone to our homes needing food, water, or whatever. How are we supposed to know if my brother was a wanted man?"

He scratched his chin and then rearranged his hat. "Didn't you see any erratic behavior?"

All were quiet, no one wanting to say anything, when Noah yelled from the car. "It was the perfect place to come. Naïve Amish have their heads buried in their Bibles."

"Noah!" Rose screamed. "Did you sell cocaine out of the house?"

"See officer? She thinks I'll make a confession right here in front of you."

"I noticed odd behavior," I admitted, "but always try to think the best of someone. Noah was awful edgy, running off all the time. Even at his *daed's* funeral."

"I'm smart," Noah boasted. "When falsely accused, I have the sense to skedaddle."

"Oh, pride comes before a fall," the officer stated flatly.

I bat my lashes in disbelief. "You're quoting scripture."

"Yes, because this is the perfect example," he said with a groan, marching up to Noah, eyes ablaze. "Where were you the day of the flood that swept away your dad along with his buggy, never to be found by any law enforcement or local help? Do you think we're that naïve?"

Noah's face reddened as if ready to bust.

The screen door squeaked open. "We found bags of it. Stuck in a mattress," one police officer yelled, carrying one-gallon plastic bags. "Cocaine and lots of it."

"Officer, we knew nothing about it," Rose exclaimed. "We Amish are the trusting type."

The elderly officer asked us all to take seats on the porch. We obeyed, and he began to ask about Noah's relationship with his father. Ivy said they were at odds but patching things up, but Serena said otherwise. "Noah hated my *daed*. Said spiteful things to us about him, all untrue. He never shed a tear when he died."

"I understand Mrs. Coblenz was in the hospital and is still recovering?" he gently asked.

"I'm still a bit weak but *gut*," Ivy stated.

"Are you sure? I don't want to startle you."

"I'm fine."

The officer motioned for someone to come out of the police car parked along the road. I was as confused as a person could be when I saw Asa running to Ivy, scooping her up in his arms. Ivy pushed him away, saying she didn't believe in ghosts, and Asa planted a kiss on her lips. "I'm alive, dear woman!"

My heart thumped out of my chest and I held my twins, willing for them to stay calm.

Ivy now clung to Asa with all her might, while the girls stared in disbelief. "Officer, he was never dead?" Serena asked.

Asa put an arm around Serena. "I was washed down the river quite a bit but was able to make it to land when my strength was almost gone. There was a hunting shack, so I thought, and I went in to get dry, but it wasn't a hunting camp." At this, Asa's face contorted, and he set his jaw firm. He motioned for the officer to take over.

"It was a place we'd been keeping an eye on, suspicious that it was a place to hide drugs. We figured we could catch the sellers since they'd be there to save their stash from the flood. And we were right. But Asa got there before us and they beat him up mighty bad. We got on the scene just before…"

"Just before?" Ivy probed.

"They were going to throw him in the river."

I cringed and didn't want to ask who 'they' were, but Rose did.

"Noah's drug partners. Dangerous folk. Asa was flown to Pittsburgh and he stayed in the head trauma unit for weeks. He slowly gained his memory while we continued our investigation. When he was well enough, we had to tell him his son, Noah, was the leader of a major drug ring."

Rose set her fists on her hips. "Why didn't you tell local Amish you found an Amish man?"

Asa lowered his head, rubbing his chin. "They cut off my beard."

"Who did?" Rose asked, spinning around to stare at the officer. "Married Amish men don't shave."

Asa tapped Rose's shoulder. "Not the police. In the cabin."

"They cut his beard and put a plaid shirt on his battered body," the officer spat out in disgust, glaring at Noah. "Tried to trick the police, but we're not so naïve!"

Asa gingerly ambled over to the car and extended a hand to Noah. "I forgive you."

Noah spit at him, another string of profanities spraying out.

Asa only nodded and said he did what he was supposed to do: forgive his enemy.

"M-my brother tried to d-drown my *daed?*" Serena stuttered.

"No, his cronies. But he knew they tried to fake Asa's death. Thought he got away with it."

Asa hugged Ivy as tears streamed down his cheeks. Rose ran to him, hugging him from behind. "My *daed* never deserved such treatment."

Asa turned to Rose, weeping, "I never deserved a *dochder* like you."

~*~

Timothy whistled as he tied the buggy to the post. He near skipped to me, throwing his hands in the air. "Ruth, we sold that wardrobe over at Yoder's for five-hundred smackaroos." He ducked as if the Almighty was going to swat him for bragging. "Can you believe it? We rent the smallest space. I'm getting a bigger one and quick."

I could barely wait to tell Timothy all that transpired over at Ivy's today while he was gone. I slid over to make room on the porch swing. "That's *wunderbar*. Sit down. I have something to tell you."

He lowered himself pensively near me. "*Bopplin* okay? Ruth, you look pale."

I gripped his hand. "Remember when I couldn't get out of my mind that Asa was still alive?"

He raised a hand to feel my forehead. "No fever."

Tears could no longer be held in check. "Asa's alive," I sputtered. "He was in the hospital."

"Come again?"

"In the hospital for brain injuries. It's a long story. Gives me a headache."

"Asa's alive? Why didn't someone send word to the Amish?" Timothy asked.

"Didn't know he was Amish. He lost his memory. Noah's a drug dealer. He was taken away by the police. It was awful!"

Timothy's chin quivered. "Asa's alive," he repeated. "Noah tried to kill him?"

I told Timothy all I knew and burst into tears yet again. Timothy held me close. "Lord help us," Timothy sighed. "That's horrible. It'll take time for Asa to recover from this."

"Ivy, too," I added. "And the girls. *Ach*, one *gut* thing was that Rose and Asa seemed to bond over the whole ordeal." I leaned my head on Timothy's shoulder. "I wish you could have seen it. Rose defended Asa when Noah insulted him." Timothy handed me his clean handkerchief and I grabbed it, burying my face in it, sobbing. He asked me to take my time, to please calm down. I did, but had to tell him, "Asa said he didn't deserve a *dochder* like Rose, or something like that. He really loves Rose!"

After I was all wrung out like a dishrag, Timothy and I swung on the porch, watching the birds swoop up to the rafters to feed their babies. We tried to talk on pleasant things, like the birds, no matter how far they migrate, always come back to the exact same spot where they were born. And then it dawned on me. "Rose is coming back to the People, I believe. She told the officer that 'We Amish' don't do this and that. I think she's turned the corner."

"Praise be, Ruth," Timothy said with feeling. "Do you realize all you've done for that family?"

I hugged his muscular arm. "It was you, too. Your friendship to Asa and showing Rose what a *gut* husband is like."

Timothy turned the conversation away from himself; he could never accept too much praise. "Remember how she yelled at me when we first met her? *Ach*, we just live for the Lord, I suppose, and see the results sometimes." Timothy got up and paced the porch and started to twiddle his thumbs, head down. "Ruth, I'm taking the money I got for the wardrobe to buy three spinning wheels. I see how your nerves are calmed by spinning and the women folk next door will need a time of healing."

I burst into tears again and Timothy thought he said something wrong. I told him it touched me that he'd help the Coblenz women, but something else was bothering me. I willed myself to calm down again and cleared my throat. I pulled the letter from my pocket. "Becky finally wrote," I near spat. "She wants me to stop writing and said Lena has made her choice. She will not contact Lena."

"That's being so pigheaded." Timothy scowled and sat next to me again.

"*Nee*, pigs are darling and smart. Becky is heartless. She can't see that the only kin she has is Lena."

Timothy snuggled up to me. "She has you, *jah*? You're like a real sister."

"I suppose because I feel so deeply for Lena when she's hurt."

"That's why I had my eye on you for nearly four years before I dared ask you to court."

"What?"

"You do have a heart. A big one. Big enough to love a man like me, blunders and all." He kissed me promptly on the lips before I could say another word. After he took my breath away, I leaned in for another. I never did understand the Amish proverb 'kissing wears out, cooking doesn't.'

~*~

Two weeks later, when the rolling hills all around me hummed with green leaves swaying in a pleasant breeze, so did five spinning wheels in my living room. Lena looked across the circle at me, motioning to Rose. We both hadn't brought it up yet. Was Lena asking me to be the mouthpiece, as usual? "Rose, you're dressed in Amish clothes. You look pretty in a prayer *kapp*."

Fulfillment was etched into her face, and then she laughed. "I was wondering when you'd bring it up, Ruth. I'm coming back to the People…isn't it plain?"

Her play on words made my watermelon belly bobble. "*Jah*, it's plain. And it makes me plain happy!"

Ivy choked back tears. "God answered all my prayers. Asa's alive and a new man. Rose is coming back to the People and knows her *daed* loves her."

I remembered the three flood victims. God loved them just as much but took them home to glory. Asa was spared for a reason…

"All your prayers answered?" Lena probed. "So, you approve of Levi now?"

Rose gasped. "What's Levi got to do with this? He's not baptized. You have to be a baptized member of the church to propose."

To everyone's surprise Ivy let out a hardy laugh. "*Ach*, Rose, we like Levi. Your *daed* and I talked about him. We had to blame someone for you leaving us. We were blaming others instead of working on ourselves."

"*Mamm*," Rose exclaimed, "don't be so hard on yourself. You promised you'd try."

Ivy nodded. "Okay. Let's just say our family is whole now, or we're making lots of progress."

Serena spoke up. "Home feels like Ruth's place now. We're all talking about our feelings and…connecting. Ruth and Timothy talk a lot and I always wondered why we didn't."

I let my spinning wheel come to a stop. "Serena Coblenz, are you saying I am an outspoken Amish woman?"

Serena doubled over laughing. "My *daed* used to say that. I never did."

Laughter echoed off the walls and we resumed spinning.

"Any news of Noah?" I ventured. "It's a pity what they put in the newspaper."

Ivy straightened, her jaw stiff. "The paper is telling the truth. Noah spent three years in jail for dealing drugs when he was in his thirties. Tried to hide among the Amish."

Lena raised a hand. "I have a question about his wife. Did she die?"

Pursing her lips with closed eyes, Ivy hesitated for a while. "He was never married. It was all a lie. A ploy to get drug money to feed his habit. Asa keeps blaming himself for being a bad *daed*, and it pains me."

"No more blaming," Rose corrected. "And we move forward, *jah*? Forgive and move forward. Job never understood why all his troubles came upon him, right Ruth?"

I near busted with pride. Lena turned to hide her tears of joy. We'd talked to Rose about Job never getting his so-called 'closure,' something Rose was big on. No, we didn't have to understand everything, just trust in a loving Heavenly Father that loves us and makes all things work together for the good. "No need for closure, Rose?"

"No, everything will be an open book when we get to glory. We see in part, now, but we'll understand fully one day."

I cocked a brow. "Rose, you sound like an evangelical."

Everyone laughed but Ivy, still nervous Rose wouldn't make it through her proving time and baptism.

That Rose would go back to New Life Church, but I didn't fret like a *mamm*. I knew with the new liberty our *Gmay* enjoyed that Rose fit in. She'd grow where she was planted, among the Amish, her roots holding firm.

We sat in silence, spinning, and I couldn't help but silently pray:

Lord, you led us here to Punxsy for a reason, I can see that now. You gave me a hunger for your Word that I just couldn't squelch. Out of the abundance of my heart I spoke, and Lord, I'm so thankful no one hushed me. Your scriptures change us. Like a tree planted by streams of water, You bring forth fruit in Your time. Praise be!

Discussion Guide

Dear Readers,

My hope for this novel is that it portrayed my relationship with my dear friend Ruth. She is with the Lord now, and my grief is much better. I feel like springtime again. Like the Bible says, "Weeping may stay for the night, but joy comes in the morning." Morning has finally come. I almost didn't finish this book because grief was still fresh, but time does heal.

Now, I'm able to remember the wonderful things about our relationship, especially her love for God's Word. She taught a Bible study in her home and my husband thought she was one of the best teachers ever. Like Lena and Ruth's little prayer time, Ruth and I had that for years. Having a prayer partners, a few people who keep you accountable and 'seem to be able to read you like a book', I believe is crucial to spiritual growth.

1. Out of all the characters in the book, who would you most want to be like and why?

2. Much is said about sheep in this novel. We raise a few sheep every year on our hobby farm. They are timid creatures until they get know our voices. John 10:27 says:

    My sheep hear my voice, and I know them, and they follow me.

    What do you think of Ruth's ability to hear that still small voice of God? Read 1 Kings 19:11-13 and discuss.

3. Many Amish can't farm today due to land prices, so they have to turn to other trades to make a living. But it's rare to find an Amish family without a garden.

    Gardening is a way of showing that you believe in tomorrow. Amish Proverb

    Gardening is on the rise in America, many saying the high-tech culture is stressing them out. Do you think there's a connection between being outdoors, close to the land, and happiness?

4. "Never did I hear of anyone eating mutton," our Amish friends in Smicksburg say. The

Amish have been living in this country since the 1700s, but they hold to their traditional recipes. Do you think family traditions helps bonds people? Makes them feel like part of a community?

5. Ruth and Lena thought life would be perfect if they were neighbors, but we all have our crosses to bear, and theirs is Asa Coblenz. He was a changed man by the love of his new neighbors, though. Is there an Asa in your life you might want to take some Friendship Bread to?

6. Timothy and Ruth wondered if bickering with Asa was right. Bishop Dan said to "Provoke one another to love and good works." Hebrews 10:24. Other Bible versions use, 'spur' or 'stir up' instead of 'provoke' one another. Is there someone annoyed by you? After asking if you've done anything wrong, maybe it's conviction. We don't like to be around people who hold a mirror up to our face, exposing that something needs changed.

7. Rose believes she needs closure about her past to move on. Lena points out that Job never knew why so much calamity came upon him, yet he went on with his life. Lena lost her parents when she was ten. Children were killed in the flash flood. Do you believe we'll find closure this side of eternity? What are some crosses you bear that baffle you? Should you stop trying to figure everything out and rest in God?

When grieving Ruth's death, this scripture was a comfort:

"Come to me, all you who labor and are heavily burdened, and I will give you rest. Take my yoke upon you, and learn from me, for I am gentle and humble in heart; and you will find rest for your souls. For my yoke is easy, and my burden is light." Matt 11:28-30

8. Ruth writes to Lena's sister, feeling deeply for her friend's estrangement. Estrangement seems to be more common in our culture. Do

you agree? Is there an estranged relationship in your life? When can you say with assurance, like Lena, "I think I've written my last letter. I need to step back and wait for God to fight for me."

The Lord shall fight for you, and ye shall hold your peace. Exodus 14:14.

9. Fear and shame caused great disfunction in Asa and Ivy's family. How did the truth set them free? How important is friendship to healing?

10. This question is just for fun. Many Amish women think their house is messy if you drop by to visit if their mop or broom is out 'where everyone will see!' I chuckle. The house looks so serene, uncluttered, but a broom is not in place? Timothy *'redd'* up (clean up in Pittsburghese) for Ruth before company arrived. Are all women alike, or do we care too much about what others think?

Ivy's Lemon Custard Pie

2 tablespoons flour

½ cup sugar

2 eggs, separated

pinch of salt

1 lemon

1½ cups milk

1 pie shell

Mix 2 tablespoons of flour with ½ cup sugar and a pinch of salt. Beat

2 egg yolks. Add the juice and grated rind of 1 lemon. Then add flour

and sugar continuing to beat. Stir in 1½ cups milk and lastly fold in

2 egg whites beaten stiff, but not dry. Pour into unbaked pie shell.

Bake in hot oven, 425 degrees for 15 minutes. Reduce heat to moderate

350 degrees and bake 15 minutes more.

Ruth's Old-Fashioned Sand Tarts

2 cups sugar

1 cup butter

4 eggs

2 ¾ flour

Work butter and part of the sugar together, then the remainder of the sugar and two eggs should be mixed in. Use flour enough to make very stiff. Roll thin, cut out in small squares, wet top with two eggs beaten, sprinkle with sugar, cinnamon and chopped almonds. Bake in moderate oven, 10 minutes.

About Author Karen Anna Vogel

Karen Anna Vogel is dusting off book outlines written thirty years ago when she was running after her four preschoolers. Having empty nest syndrome, she delved into writing. Many books and novellas later, she's passionate about portraying the Amish and small-town life in a realistic way. Being a "Trusted English Friend" to Amish in rural Western Pennsylvania and New York, she writes what she's experienced, many novels based on true stories. She also blogs at *Amish Crossings*

She's a graduate of Seton Hill University, majoring in Psychology & Elementary Education, and Andersonville Theological Seminary with a Masters in Biblical Counseling. Karen's a yarn hoarder not in therapy, knitting or crocheting something at all times. This passion leaks into her books along with hobby farming and her love of dogs. Her husband of thirty-seven years is responsible for turning her into a content country bumpkin.

Visit her at www.karenannavogel.com/contact

Karen's booklist so far (2018)
Check her Amazon author page for updates.
Continuing Series:
Amish Knitting Circle: Smicksburg Tales 1
Amish Knitting Circle: Smicksburg Tales 2
Amish Knit Lit Circle: Smicksburg Tales 3
Amish Knit & Stitch Circle: Smicksburg Tales 4

Amish Knit & Crochet Circle: Smicksburg 5
Standalone Novels:
Knit Together: Amish Knitting Novel
The Amish Doll: Amish Knitting Novel
Plain Jane: A Punxsutawney Amish Novel
Amish Herb Shop Series:
Herbalist's Daughter Trilogy
Herbalist's Son Trilogy
At Home in Pennsylvania Amish Country Series:
Winter Wheat
Spring Seeds
Summer Haze (Yet to be released)
Autumn Grace (Yet to be released)
Novellas:
Amish Knitting Circle Christmas: Granny & Jeb's Love Story
Amish Pen Pals: Rachael's Confession
Christmas Union: Quaker Abolitionist of Chester County, PA
Love Came Down at Christmas
Love Came Down at Christmas 2
Love Came Down at Christmas 3
Non-fiction:
31 Days to a Simple Life the Amish Way
A Simple Christmas the Amish Way

How to Know the Love of God

God so loved the world, that He gave His only Son, that whoever believes in Him should not perish but have eternal life. *John 3:16*

God so loved the world

God loves you!

"I have loved you with an everlasting love." — Jeremiah 31:3
"Indeed the very hairs of your head are numbered." — Luke 12:7

That He gave His only Son
Who is God's son?

"Jesus answered, 'I am the way and the truth and the life. No one comes to the Father except through me.'" — John 14:6

That whoever believes in Him

Whosoever? Even me?

No matter what you've done, God will receive you into His family. He will change you, so come as you are.

"I am the Lord, the God of all mankind. Is anything too hard for me?"
— Jeremiah 32:27

"The Spirit of the Lord will come upon you in power, … and you will be changed into a different person." — 1 Samuel 10:6

Should not perish but have eternal life

Can I have that "blessed hope" of spending eternity with God?

"I write these things to you who believe in the name of Son of God so that you may know that you have eternal life." - 1 John 5:13

To know Jesus, come as you are and humbly admit you're a sinner. A sinner is someone who has missed the target of God's perfect holiness. I think we all qualify to be sinners. Open the door of your heart and let Christ in. He'll cleanse you from all sins. He says he stands at the door of your heart and knocks. Let Him in. Talk to Jesus like a friend…because when you open the door of your heart, you have a friend eager to come inside.

Bless you!
If you have any questions, contact Karen at
www.karenannavogel.com